Praise for the 13 Reasons for Murder Series

"…hard to put down and am keen to read the next in the series."—Reader's Favorite 5-Star

"Full of sass, good friends, and a bit of blood, this novel was a joy to read."—Julie E.

"…suspenseful, addictive…hope there are more books with this character."—BookBub Review

"I look forward to…learning more about Britney."—Studiohnh.com Review

"…oddly addictive…cannot wait for the next book…"—Amazon.ca Review

"…flows at a quick pace and leaves you wanting more…" —Goodreads Review

"The plot is fresh and unique, a nice change to read something a little different…"—Reader's Favorite 4-Star

"…well written and kept me on the edge of my seat…"—Heather W.

13 Reasons for Murder: Bad Blood

13 Reasons for Murder #5

Amanda Byrd

Blacksheep Press

Contents

About the Author VII

Chapter 1

1. One 3

2. Two 9

3. Three 15

4. Four 23

5. Five 29

6. Six 37

7. Seven 43

8. Eight 51

9. Nine 59

10. Ten 67

11. Eleven 77

12. Twelve 87

13. Thirteen 93

14. Fourteen — 103

15. Fifteen — 111

16. Sixteen — 117

17. Seventeen — 127

18. Eighteen — 133

19. Nineteen — 141

20. Twenty — 149

21. Twenty-One — 157

22. Twenty-Two — 163

23. Twenty-Three — 169

24. Twenty-Four — 175

25. Twenty-Five — 181

26. Twenty-Six — 189

27. Twenty-Seven — 195

Acknowledgments — 202

Also by Amanda Byrd — 204

About the
Author

Amanda has a love of horror and borderline obsession with fictional serial killers. She frequently makes *Hannibal*, *Harry Potter*, and *Dexter* references in "normal" conversation. She is also a full-time psychology major. When not writing, Amanda can be found reading, playing video games, or watching shows and movies like *Mindhunter*, *Hannibal*, *Harry Potter,* or *Dexter*. Amanda currently resides in Tampa, Florida with her husband and two cats.

Follow Amanda online: www.amandabyrd.net
Sign up for the monthly email list and get a free story

For Harvey, as always. My support that I can't always see or hear.

One

THE NEWS HAD BEEN everywhere the past few weeks. Michael Williamson had been arrested in the disappearance of Sally Walker, also known as Shaelyn White. After talking to an informant, the DA had also charged him with witness intimidation, drug trafficking, and money laundering. Even if he magically beat the eventual murder rap, Michael Williamson was going to spend a very long time in a very hot, very dangerous Florida state prison.

"The judge denied bail for Williamson, calling him a flight risk…"

I was in the kitchen making myself a cocktail while listening for the weather. When I heard that last line, I snorted. Would this be what happened to me if Stu told anyone?

I had been feeling a combination of anxiety and extreme sadness lately. Having not heard a word from Stu made life that much more unbearable. The only consolation was running into Andrew York a few weeks ago. That guy made me feel something *other* than sad.

The clock read 9:23 a.m. I sipped my dirty martini while judging myself for drinking so early in the day. I shook my head; I deserved to wallow in this pain. I deserved the pain too.

It had been two weeks since Stu left. Two weeks of nightmares, tears, and alcohol. I'd barely eaten anything. The girls were worried about me too.

We'd had a dinner night since then and I'd looked like a train wreck. My hair has been a mess, I'd worn no makeup, and my eyes were so puffy they wondered how I'd driven myself there. Kristen and Danielle had stopped by almost every day since. But today was for me. I needed to be alone.

I picked up the shaker and walked out onto the patio. The weather was offensive, even for Florida in September. I sat down and poured more into my glass. I sipped and stared out toward the lake. Beyond that was a such thick haze, the buildings on the other side were hard to make out.

"With a heat index over 105…" floated out from the living room. That made me stop caring about what weather was in store.

I snorted then slid the door closed. Minion didn't need to feel the soup. Neither did my electric bill by keeping the door open.

There were no sounds other than traffic and sirens. It was a typical Saturday.

I finished the remaining martini and sighed. The sweat from the shaker was now a puddle on the table. And the sweat from my face flowed onto my shirt. I felt sticky and slimy at the same time. I'd showered once already and now needed another. I snorted again and pulled myself up before opening the door to a cat who showed her annoyance that she hadn't been outside with me.

"It's gross out there," I told her as I closed the door.

I rinsed out the shaker and glass, then set them on a towel on the counter. I'd be using them both again soon, and had no care for cleanliness.

I walked into the living room and fell onto the couch. The weather guy was just finishing, and the seven-day was on-screen. There was some relief in sight, with rain in the forecast all day tomorrow. That meant jogging would be soggy. Like my current disposition. I closed my eyes and let his voice soothe my mind. Then my phone vibrated on the table, extracting a growl and snort from me.

I opened my eyes as I sat up and leaned forward to pick my phone up. Kristen was calling. I pressed the power button to mute the call and set it back down on the table. I knew I couldn't avoid my friends—or my life—forever. But for today, I really wanted to be alone. I needed it.

I flipped one of the streaming services on and scrolled for a horror movie that always made me feel better. *The Devil's Rejects* was always good for at least one giggle. One of the actors was also a comedian and brought that to one of the scenes. For years I hated it, but it was amusing—I loved the violence—so it grew on me.

But not today. I advanced through the beginning to *that* scene…and felt nothing. Not even the tiniest bit of mirth. I stopped the movie, stood, and shuffled into the kitchen for more alcohol.

The bottle of vodka I'd been keeping on the counter was gone. I peeked into the recycling bin and saw it lying on top. I supposed I'd finished it just a bit ago and didn't remember. So I searched the cabinets and pantry for another bottle. There wasn't one.

"Shit."

Minion paused her bathing long enough to eye me like I'd called her names. I petted her. She licked my hand, then nuzzled it away from her. Even my cat wanted nothing to do with me. Not that I could blame her.

I plopped onto a chair at the table and sighed heavily. I needed to get myself out of this funk somehow. And the liquor store didn't open until 11 a.m. anyway.

Sighing again, I leaned forward and rested my elbows on my knees. I tried to think of something I could do now that would ease the anxiety. The only thing I came up with was to go for a jog. Maybe that would help clear the booze from my brain, at the very least.

I changed and headed out. I took a spiral sort of route in an effort to challenge myself. And to beat myself into mental submission. I knew if I hurt enough from the jog, I would push harder mentally. The chain reaction would then cause my mind to retaliate with anger, or something like it. Then I might be able to find my way out of the wet paper bag I'd now found myself in.

Earbuds in, I walked across Bayshore to the bay. I berated myself until I reached the railing. Then I questioned everything while I stretched. What the hell was I thinking telling Stu? What had I hoped to accomplish? It couldn't have been to bring him closer. Did I want to go to prison?

I sighed, changed the song, and hit the pavement. I swirled my neighborhood for thirty minutes, maybe more. I didn't care about the distance or time, only how I felt. And I felt like I'd been run over.

My whole body ached. It should have. I hadn't jogged or stretched for days. I did nothing more than go to work, drink, and sleep. Sleep was my number one next to Minion. I ate a little between those things too. But it didn't grasp me like the booze and sleep did.

I appreciated stress eating, but it wasn't what I went through these past few weeks. Instead, I stressed and didn't eat. I'd lost a bit of weight too, which should have worried me but didn't. I cared about almost nothing.

My phone vibrated in the holder strapped to my arm as I walked into my house. Without looking, I pressed the button on the earbud wire, answering the call.

"Hi. Is this Britney Cage?"

Two

"Mᴀʏ I ᴀsᴋ ᴡʜᴏ's calling?" I asked, pretending to be my assistant, Barb.

The man on the other end chuckled. "Hey, Brit. It's Andrew."

Ugh, gross. This asshole. I took a deep breath and attempted to sound happy.

"Hey, Andrew! What's up? How are you?"

"I'm well, thanks. Do you still own Passing Through?"

"I do." I knew where this was headed, and I didn't like it.

"Can you help me out? I need something short-term until I find a new job. Unless the firm I temp at wants me full time, obviously." His tone was snobbish, like it always had been. Like he was doing *me* a favor by letting me employ him.

"Sure. Come in Monday and fill out the paperwork. Bring your bank info, résumé, and two forms of ID." I sounded like a robot. Plus, I felt like he may have already known what he needed to bring.

"Already have it all together and ready to go. Thanks, Brit! I really appreciate it!"

"No problem," I said as the metaphorical light bulb dinged in my brain. "Have a good weekend, Andrew."

As I took the earbuds out of my ears, I realized something seemingly insignificant. How convenient it was that the five people I'd killed in the last two years had all temped for me at some point? I smirked and hoped the cops wouldn't put it together for a long time from now or I'd be screwed.

I pulled my phone from the holder as I unstrapped it, and walked upstairs for a shower. As I went, I scrolled through my last text conversation with Stu.

Sorry about her. She just transferred from some county further south. Anyway, I told her about Michael, and she's got others helping her track him down. One of the CIs said they saw him around town.

No worries. She was polite. I'm worried about Shae though.

I don't think we'll find her.

You think he killed her, don't you?

We can talk about this later.

Okay. Wanna come over for dinner and a movie?

Brit, you only need tell me the time.

6.

K. See you soon.

My eyes misted over. Then I got mad and threw my phone onto my bed. It bounced off the headboard before landing between a couple of pillows. I sighed, grateful that it was a Samsung.

I undressed and flung my clothes into the laundry bin and got in the shower. I hadn't bothered to start the water before getting in, either. It was like I wanted to feel the sting of the ice water goosebumps. The water ran warm almost immediately after the initial shock. Or maybe it just felt that way because my skin was used to it in a weird way. I thought there was a word for it, but my brain failed me.

Under the water that suddenly flowed hot, I stood, letting it wash over me. As it did, I let myself get angry. Angry for actually thinking I could tell Stu and not suffer any repercussions. Angry for even wanting to tell him in the first place. Angry for letting my feelings for him get in the way. Then I smirked.

"It worked," I said out loud. "Today is the day I get my shit together and get back to being me. Besides, I have a murder to plan."

I washed and got out, towel-drying my hair after. I would be home all day. Which meant I could spend the day researching. I wanted to savor this one though. It all had to be perfect. The planning, anyway.

My why was straightforward because Andrew was, well, Andrew. After one misguided romp, he believed he could have me whenever he wanted. If he was like that with me, I imagined he'd been the same way with other women. I wasn't sure which pissed me off more. But that added to why he needed to die.

The how was also much simpler now that I had my custom knife. I considered giving it a name, but that would likely have made me grow even more attached to it than I already was. It was a tool that, if necessary, could be replaced. Naming it might make it harder to let go of in an emergency. I hadn't planned to keep it forever, either. I just wanted to keep it for as long as I could. For as long as I killed without being caught.

I put on an outfit that would be called lounge wear. It consisted of pair of terry pants and an oversize top. It was comfortable. I never understood why the term *lounge wear* even existed. It wasn't like I would be actually lounging. Or wearing it to a lounge. Were those things even still around?

I swiped my phone from the bed where it had landed earlier and headed for the stairs. It vibrated for a second to remind me there was a notification to check. I unlocked it and saw the text message icon had a number two on it. I tapped it to see who needed to text me twice in about a half hour.

It was Julie.

Hey, Brit. I hope you're okay.

I love you. Let me know if you need anything.

I smiled. Julie had always been good to me. And far too kind. Not just to me, but to others as well.

Thanks. Be in the office tomorrow. Love you too.

Placing the phone in my pocket, I went downstairs and started scanning the streaming channels for serial killer movies. The ones I was looking for today were the ones with creative body disposal. That was the sole criteria. I found one within a few minutes.

Ashley Judd and Morgan Freeman were in it. I enjoyed watching movies Judd was in, especially. And Freeman was an amazing actor. So what if this movie was made in the '90s? I thought the ones she was in were good. It was a bonus that there was a serial killer—or two—in this one. I scrolled to the thumbnail and let the screen stay there while I went into the kitchen to grab a snack and drink.

In the fridge, there was half a bottle of red moscato and some cheese cubes. The combination looked more enticing than anything else did. I pulled the bottle and container out and set them on the counter. There wasn't much sense in wasting a glass for that small amount of wine, but I used one anyway.

Back in the living room, I pressed play. Then I sipped and munched and enjoyed the movie. I got to the part where one of the killers left a victim's body tied to a tree. I thought that part was odd, along with the fact that there were two working together. The other killer left no bodies out in the open. At least none that were mentioned. So much for research. At least the movie was tolerable.

After it ended, I got to thinking. I decided that tying a dead body to a tree was a cry for help; to be caught, not to taunt the police. I wasn't going down *that* road. I had no desire to be caught. Nor did I delude myself into thinking I would *never* be caught. Sure, I'd told Stu. But that was out of a want to be honest with him. Not because I'd held some secret desire to face a death sentence.

Watching *Dexter*, however, got my brain going.

Three

I SCROLLED THROUGH MY watch list until I found it, and pressed play once again. This show was a good one. And it was full of useful information. I'd sort of used bits and pieces before, so to have it influence me now wasn't a surprise. Besides, he had it right: hide who you really are from your family, friends, and other loved ones.

I'd made it halfway through season three when it finally hit me. He cut the bodies up, put the pieces in plastic bags, then dumped them into the ocean. In the Gulf Stream, to be precise. The bit I found odd was the plastic bags. They didn't dissolve, so why bother with them? Why not hold them overboard and—

I giggled maliciously. My disposal method for this kill was solidified. But I wasn't going to dismember another body so soon. I didn't even have a different way to accomplish that. It wasn't worth it this time.

What I would need was a reliable way to hoist a body, though. I couldn't remember if that shop in Ybor had an engine hoist. If it did, all I needed was a way to transport it to a dock at night. My plans were coming together more solidly than they had for Shae.

But I'd also need a boat capable of going out to sea. *Shit*. Maybe Andrew had one and I didn't know about it. I found myself hoping that was the case. But would life give me this kill that easily?

Then I mentally listed some other things I didn't already have and would need to acquire. The list wasn't long or expensive. It was more like it was an odd list for someone who wasn't a researcher, construction worker, or contractor of sorts. But when had that ever been an issue?

I stopped the show and checked my phone for the time. I hadn't realized that I'd been watching things for as long as I had been. At least Minion hadn't realized what time it was yet. I figured I'd beat her to it and headed into the kitchen, calling her name as I walked.

I fed her, then checked the fridge and pantry for my dinner. There wasn't much that would cook quickly. I sighed and slid the notepad and pen I kept on the counter over to me, writing my grocery list out. I didn't even have pasta in the house. How sad.

Back in the living room, I ordered a pizza, Hawaiian style. It was the one with barbecue sauce instead of marinara It also had ham, bacon, and pineapple. I was a monster in all forms of the word, but especially for my pizza choice. And I almost took pride in that. The app said it would be at my door in about an hour. I set my phone down and started the show back up to pass the time.

The timing of my food arrival coincided with a knock on my beloved serial killer's door. I paused it and got up to get my dinner. I wished the delivery girl a good night and set the box on the coffee table. Plates weren't necessary, but I needed a napkin. I grabbed one from the kitchen and sat back down to savor this rare treat.

I unpaused the episode and dug into my cheesy goodness. If I hadn't had the feelings issues earlier, I'd have thought this was the perfect way to spend a lazy day. That aside, tonight was shaping up to be the kind I appreciated. Minion even joined me as the episode ended.

The time on my phone read 8:49. It was getting close to bedtime. I stroked Minion's head and scratched her chin while deciding if I wanted to watch one more episode. The answer was obvious.

When the next episode finished, I closed the app and shut the TV off. I shifted Minion and stood, carrying the pizza box to the kitchen. I'd eaten half and would take the other half to the office tomorrow. I put the remaining slices in a plastic container and stuck it in the fridge. Then I washed the glasses I'd left in and around the sink. This was the last night of feeling sorry for myself.

By the time I'd made it to my bed, Minion was already there. She sat on my pillow wearing a look of disapproval. I giggled and nudged her aside as I crawled in. I was comfy and asleep as soon as I pulled the blanket up.

· • • ● ● • ● ● • • ·

My alarm went off like any other day. But my brain overrode my heart, just like it had long ago. I'd almost forgotten what it was like to wake up and start my day without a care in the world. I smiled and enjoyed it for a moment before getting out of bed.

The sun shone in the bathroom when I brushed my teeth, reflecting off the brushed nickel door handle. It blinded me a bit, and made me wonder how gross the weather was. Not that it mattered; Florida weather usually wasn't ideal until November anyway.

I changed out of my pajamas and into jogging gear, then stretched before leaving. I was still sore from yesterday, though not as badly as I'd expected. The stretching felt great. It reminded me that, like my body, I was capable of great things. I smiled and headed out.

I took the same swirl pattern I'd taken before. Not to avoid anyone, but because the route was pretty and a little bit more of a challenge than my usual. Though I was glad that if Andrew had been out on Bayshore, it was likely we wouldn't bump into each other. After all, it was on a jog that I'd recently run into him. And had decided my next kill. I should have been grateful to the fates for that, and I was. But I didn't want to see him before our meeting at my office.

I rounded the corner onto my street and slowed as I reached my house. The nosy old bat was outside, and she waved to me. I smiled and waved back, then pointed to my wrist, indicating I was pressed for time. She smiled and nodded an acknowledgment before turning to go back inside. Did I really care about what she wanted? She would have come knocking if there were a true emergency or problem, so I brushed it off.

I showered and got ready for the day, feeling like a new version of myself. I stood looking at my reflection in the full-length mirror. I took in all that was me: my body, my faults, clothes, hair…I smiled, liking what I saw and how I felt in my skin. It was good to be back to an ice queen of sorts. Sure, I still cared about my friends and family, but I was done letting romantic feelings get in my way. I made the rules, and this was my world to live in.

I'd half expected a police cruiser to be waiting at the office for me when I arrived. I breathed relief when I pulled in and didn't see one. Barb's car was the only one here. If I was half an hour early, how much earlier had she gotten here?

I parked and went inside. Barb was coming back from the hallway with a cup of coffee in her hand.

"Good morning!" She beamed. "How are you, Britney?"

"I'm well, thanks! What time did you get here?"

"Just a few minutes ago. It's Monday and you've been…busy. So I figured I'd get started a little earlier than usual." Her tone revealed her concern, but it didn't take the glow from her face.

"Thank you. I really appreciate it. How are you?" I asked, smiling devilishly. "If you glow any more, I'm afraid you'll melt!"

Barb blushed and giggled. "Aw, thanks. I'm great."

She looked at me, and I saw the internal debate going through her mind. I smiled and opened the door to my office, walking in. She'd tell me if she wanted to.

I hung my purse on the coat rack and put my cardigan on. I didn't care about anyone seeing the artwork on my arms, but it was always a little chilly in here. As I booted up my computer, Barb came in and stood behind a chair, hands on the back.

"What's up?" I asked her, looking up from entering my password.

"He asked me to move in with him!" She squealed. Her face somehow lit up even more.

I put on a large grin. "Congratulations! Wait, you *did* say yes, didn't you?"

"YES!" Her shriek echoed a little, causing me to wince. "Oh my God, I'm so sorry!"

I giggled. "It's okay. You're excited. You have every reason to be. I'm so happy for you! Do you need time off? If you need to go look at places or—"

Barb held a hand up, still smiling. "Not yet. But maybe soon." She walked around the chair she was holding on to and sat in it. I sat in mine, keeping the friendly appearance I'd always had with her.

"But..." I nudged.

"But I'm nervous."

"That's totally normal. Julie was nervous when she and Cody moved in together too. Why don't you ask her to chat with you about how to cope with the nerves?"

"Would she? I mean, I don't really know her like that."

"She will. She's a really great person; you'll see." I kept a smile on my face while assuring her Julie would be a good source of advice.

"Cool. I'll email her," Barb said, standing. "Thanks, Brit!"

She turned and started to walk out, but turned back to me when she reached the doorway. "You sure you're okay?"

I nodded. "I am."

She nodded and smiled, then walked back to her desk.

The front door chimed.

I looked at the clock in the bottom corner of my computer screen. We weren't open yet.

My mind started to race.

Four

I HEARD A MAN address Barb. His voice was low, and I couldn't make out who he said he was or what he wanted. My palms clammed up. I chewed on the inside of my lip. And I waited.

The phone on my desk rang and I picked it up.

"Andrew York is here to see you, Ms. Cage," Barb said.

I let out an audible sigh. "Thank you. I'll be right out."

I stood and walked into my private bathroom. I washed the sweat off my hands and let the fear drain from my face. I guessed I wasn't fully my old self after all. But I would be soon enough.

I straightened my clothes, took a deep breath, painted a smile on, and walked out to greet Andrew.

"Andrew, hi!" I said, eying him from head to toe. Andrew was the same height as me, and not bad to look at. He was thin but fit. His long brownish-black hair shone, and his blue eyes sparkled. "You clean up nice."

He smiled and stuck a hand out. I grasped it and shook. "Thanks, Brit. So do you."

"Let's go back into my office for a few minutes," I said. He handed me a folder as I spoke.

He winked at me, and it took all of my strength to not make a disgusted sound out loud. I turned and walked back to my desk, Andrew following.

"Open or closed?" he asked, standing in the doorway.

"Open, please," I replied, sitting in my chair.

"Okay," he said. His face drooped a little. I smirked as I opened the folder he'd handed me in the reception area.

I sifted through the papers as Andrew sat down. I made noises of approval and nodded while he watched me. I closed the folder when I finished.

"Everything looks good," I said, smiling. I opened a new database entry and started to type in his name. "When can you start? What's the pay rate you're looking for? Job title?"

We went over all the important stuff, including his basic info that I could have used his résumé for. I wasn't trying to be lazy; it was just smoother this way. When I was done entering what I needed to match him, I let him know he still had to go out to one of the cubicles for the rest of the on-boarding.

Andrew exaggerated his frown. "Do I really?" he pled.

"Yes," I answered. "If you have any questions, Barb can help you. Welcome aboard."

I stood, shook his hand, and led him to the door-way.

"Thanks again," he said, flashing me that mischie-vous grin he used to get women.

"You're welcome. I might have something for you by the time you leave," I told him.

He sat and got started with his on-boarding and I walked over to Barb.

She didn't immediately look away from her screen as she typed, but she knew I was there. "What can I do for you?"

"Please let me know when Andrew is finished."

"Sure thing," Barb replied as she turned to smile at me.

I nodded my thanks and walked back into my of-fice. I sat down at my computer and looked up the placement I'd had in mind for Andrew. It was at the same firm I'd sent Jim, Barb's boyfriend, to. If anyone could put Andrew in his place—not the place I'd be putting him, of course—it would be Jim. The opening was for a junior accountant who reported directly to Jim.

I picked up the phone on my desk and dialed the number for Jim. He answered after two rings.

"Hey, babe!" he said.

"Hey babe yourself, buddy," I retorted.

"Oh…shit. I'm sorry Ms. Cage." I could feel the heat from his red face through the phone.

I giggled. "Jim, I'm kidding. Sorry, I thought you might have picked up on that. Anyway, are you still looking for a junior accountant?"

"I am. You have someone for me?"

"I do. An old friend from college. Look, he's a special case. I don't want you giving him any preferential treatment. If anything, be harder on him than anyone else. He's looking for permanent employment too. So don't be afraid to test him out just because I know the guy. Know what I mean?"

"Sure do. Thanks, Ms. Cage. Email me his info, please? Sorry to cut you short, but I have a meeting in about three minutes."

"You got it, Jim. Talk soon."

I hung up the phone and sent the information Jim requested. Then I walked out into the reception area, where Andrew was finishing the data entry part of the hiring process.

"I sent your info over to a CFO who needs a junior accountant. He'll be calling you today," I informed him.

Barb side-eyed me as I said that. She knew which job I'd put him in for. She gave Andrew a polite smile and went back to typing.

"Thanks, Brit. I really appreciate your help," Andrew said.

"No problem. Have a good day. Any other questions before I get back to it?"

"Nope."

"Awesome," I said. "See you later."

Back in my office, I realized how awful this arrangement would be until I got back to the old me, the one who had no feelings of guilt or remorse. Or of generally feeling bad for being a fraud. I sat back down, sighed, and got back to work.

I spent the next few hours until lunch replying to emails. One of them was to Julie about a contract with a client. Apparently, the client wanted to modify it via Julie's good graces, not legally. I told her to inform the client to go through me since those decisions weren't for her to make. I also asked her how she felt about agreeing to what the client wanted. I valued her input more than I realized. It didn't matter that she was the one to bring this particular client on or that she was the one who interacted with them the most.

The next thing I knew, Barb was in the doorway saying something about going to lunch.

"Oh shit!" I looked away from my screen to Barb. "I didn't even realize the time!"

She smiled. "So do you want anything?"

"No, thanks. I have some leftover pizza," I replied.

"Okay. See you in an hour," she chirped.

"Bye."

I walked to my purse to grab the container of pizza. I reached inside and discovered it wasn't there.

"Well, shit. Looks like I'll be going home for lunch today," I muttered.

I shrugged and went back to work until Barb returned from her lunch.

"Barb," I called when she'd walked back in.

"Yes?"

"I left my lunch at home. So, I'm just going to finish the day working there. If you need me…"

"You got it, Brit. Is there anything you need done before you go?"

"Nah. Thanks though. Do you need me for anything?"

"Not that I can think of. Unless something came in while I was gone…" I heard her clacking away at the keyboard.

I shut my computer down and grabbed my things before walking out. As I opened my mouth to say goodbye, Barb beat me to it.

"Brit? I've got an email here from Julie's client who wanted to circumvent you. Julie blind copied me on it." Her tone quivered a bit.

"Okay, no worries. I'll bcc you in my reply to Julie. Have a good night, Barb."

I stepped out into the bright, soupy weather and felt something land on my shoulder.

Five

I TURNED MY HEAD to see what it was. A pile of whiteish-gray goo sat there.

"Fucking seagulls."

I spun around and opened the door. My head was cocked to the side a bit in an effort to keep the droppings from my face. Barb looked up when she heard the door chime, and a curious look spread across her face.

"Um, are you okay?"

"Yeah, I need to use the bathroom though. No sooner did the door close behind me than a seagull dropped the remnants of its lunch on my shoulder," I said, walking down the hall to the main bathroom.

I flipped the light on and wet a paper towel. In minutes, I'd gotten it off, but there was still a slight stain. I sighed, turned the light off, and walked out.

"Did you get it?" Barb asked.

"Mostly. Good thing I've got a selection of shirts in my Jeep. This one is being dropped at the cleaners on the way home." I smirked.

"You can use dish liquid and—oh. That's a satin top. Never mind," Barb said, suddenly embarrassed.

"If it ever happens again, I'll ask for you to finish telling me that tip," I said trying to help her feel better. "Besides, isn't the old wives' tale that it's good luck or something?"

"That's what my mom always told me," she replied, her skin tone returning to normal.

"Then I'll take it that way." I shrugged. "Okay, I'm really leaving now."

"Bye," Barb called as I was halfway out the door. I waved back and walked to my Jeep.

I opened the back and pulled a shirt from the duffle bag of clothes I'd kept there. It didn't match my skirt, but that didn't matter to me. The shirt that had been shit on was one of my favorites, and I needed the stain gone.

I laid the dirty top on the front passenger seat with the shit shoulder hanging off. Then I hopped in the driver's seat and left.

The dry cleaner wasn't quite on my route home, but it was close to my house. I stopped and dropped the shirt off, holding the ticket in my hand as I climbed back into my Jeep. The lady inside laughed when she saw the airbrushed mouse head on the front of the shirt I had on. I joined in her laughter; I did look stupid. She told me that in her home country of Russia, it was considered good luck to be pooped on by a bird.

"And all this time I thought that was a made-up American story to help those pooped on feel better," I remarked.

She smiled. "Ah who knows. My mother told me that when I was growing up, long before we came to America. See you in a few days," she finished.

I left wondering why I'd never known it was a Russian superstition too. I paused for a moment longer, then shrugged, and went on my way.

I was home in a handful of minutes.

As I backed into my driveway, the lady across the street came out of her front door. *Stalk much, lady? Damn.* No sooner had my feet hit concrete than was she in my face.

"Britney, how are you?" She asked.

"Fine, thanks. You?" I locked the Jeep and armed the alarm. The horn sounded and made her jump a bit. I held back a smirk.

"I'm well," she said in her snobbish way, with a fake smile. "Look, I know you've had issues in the past. I just want to make sure—"

"Don't worry. I've stopped attracting stalkers for now. I can't promise that another one won't pop up, though. Maybe you should move to an assisted living facility with armed security? Or you could just stay the fuck out of my business. I never heard you complain when my cop friends were over," I spat. Then it dawned on me. "Ohhh, I get it. You don't want the HOA to have to pay for security or an officer. I hate to be the bearer of bad news," the venom dripped from my teeth, "but we don't have a crime issue here. We have a nosy people issue. Now get off my property."

A look of hurt flashed across her face. But only for a second. Then it hardened before she stomped off.

I knew private property laws were skewed when it came to associations, but damned if I'd let her use my friends for her own made-up purposes. Besides, it wasn't like Stu came over with his patrol car often anyway.

I was annoyed. If I didn't like this area so much, I'd have left a while ago. But it was convenient and relatively calm. There weren't many children around; it was mostly retirees living in this neighborhood. She was also a retiree. And she'd told me on more than one occasion that she had nothing else better to do. Apparently, harassing people for no reason was fun for her.

My thoughts raced as I changed into something more comfortable. I wanted to shut that geriatric bitch up permanently. But I also knew doing so would put me in a spotlight worse than being stalked.

I finished changing and went back downstairs to where my laptop waited. I poured a glass of water before sitting down and getting back to work.

When I opened the lid and pressed the power button, nothing happened. So I pressed it again.

"DAMMIT!" I yelled, causing Minion to tear off up the stairs.

I went to the guest room closet, hoping I'd left the charging cord in there. Opening the door, I found it was wrapped neatly and placed in one of the door storage baskets. I sighed in relief and picked it up. Maybe the day was starting to turn back around. As I closed the door, my phone rang.

I tried to say no and fuck off, but they came out at the same time. "No-off," I said. Then burst into giggle fits. As long as I could still laugh while fighting anger, annoyance, and lingering sadness, I knew I'd be okay.

I plugged the laptop in then checked to see whose call I'd missed. It was from Julie. She'd left a voicemail, but I didn't care to listen to it. Instead, I called her back.

"Passing Through Temp Agency, can you hold please?" she said.

I smiled as I heard the hold music. It was some classical thing the phone company provided. It was also calming.

"Thanks for holding. How can I help you?"

"Hey, Jules. You called?"

"Hi, Britney! I did. Did you get my message?"

"No, I figured I'd just call you back. What's going on?"

For the next forty-some minutes, Julie and I discussed the contract that her client was trying to change.

"I know, that's why I sent it to you and Barb," she said. "He's a real piece of work. He thinks just because I'm nice that I'm also naive." She huffed.

"No offense, but you can be. Though I haven't seen you be when it comes to work. Just your personal life," I giggled.

"Wow, Brit. Because you're *never* naive in your personal affairs," she jabbed at me.

I sucked in a breath through clenched teeth. I knew she wasn't trying to be a bitch; she was just being defensive.

"I'm sorry, Julie. I wasn't trying to be mean," I said. I meant it too.

"I know. I'm sorry too. I'm just so frustrated! So, how do you wanna handle this?"

"Now that he's refusing reasonable accommodations, I'm sending it to the lawyer. Then my lawyer will send it to his lawyer. *With* all of the emails, so send them to me, okay? I'm done playing games." I snorted. I had no tolerance for anyone trying to take advantage of Julie's kind nature. And I certainly had even less tolerance for those trying to fuck me and my company over. It was time to sic the lawyers on this guy.

"You got it," Julie replied. "Dinner soon?"

"Definitely! How does Thursday sound?" I asked, flipping through the planner that sat next to me.

"Let me double-check Brian's therapy schedule, and I'll let you know." There was a crashing sound in the background. "Shit. Brit, I gotta go. Damned dog—"

The line went dead. I giggled. Though I didn't know why she'd taken Applesauce into the office, I was amused that he'd gotten Julie to cuss.

I pressed the power button on the laptop, and this time it booted up. I knew it would be a few minutes before I could use it, so I took the time to pull my lunch from the fridge. Then I inhaled the first slice. I didn't care that it was cold; cold pizza had always been a vice of mine. The second, and final, slice didn't stand a chance either. I dropped the container into the sink to be washed later.

By then, the laptop had finished its boot sequence and was ready for me to use it. It had even charged quite a bit more. I opened the email software and typed a lengthy one to my lawyer. I included screenshots of the emails Julie had forwarded, along with mentioning I'd forward them along separately. Overall, it took about ten minutes before I was able to send it all off.

I briefly considered stabbing this particular client, but too many people were already involved in this stupid squabble. And it really was stupid. All he wanted was to change how many temps we send him at one time, instead of just trying to negotiate new rates. His whole business was based on temporary employees. I always thought it was just an easy way to get out of paying health insurance and all that. I mean, it wasn't a terrible idea. It was just more costly.

I finished typing and hit the send button. That was likely the excitement of the day. Maybe even the next few months. Until I did away with Andrew.

Then my doorbell rang.

Six

I KEPT PLAYING AROUND in my email inbox, purposely not making any noise.

The bell rang again, followed by a woman's voice.

"I know you're in there, dumbass! Your Jeep is in the driveway!"

It was Kristen.

"It's open!" I called.

The door opened and closed. I heard squeaking on the floor as Kristen walked farther inside. When she reached me, she wrapped me in a hug.

"I stopped by the office, but Barb said you came home. You okay?" She went to the fridge, opened it, and took the orange juice out. I giggled as she poured herself a glass and sat across from me at the table.

"Well? "she prodded.

"I'm fine. I forgot my lunch, so I figured I'd just work from home. No big deal." I shrugged.

She looked my face over, then into my eyes. "Well, your face no longer gives you away. Or not right now anyway. I'll believe you. But if that changes, you promise to tell me? I mean it. You've been so sad…"

"I know. And I'm sorry for not talking about it and worrying. It's just that Stu and I had a huge fight and I haven't heard from him in weeks. I'm slowly coming to terms with the fact that we may never speak again." I faked a smile; it still hurt like hell.

"You never really said what happened. You want to talk about it?" Kristen genuinely cared. We'd been friends for nearly twelve years now and told each other everything. Almost everything.

"Not really. But I will if it means you'll get off my back about it." I tried to sound like an annoyed teenager, but a grin broke my face.

Kristen laughed. "Nice try. Seriously, I'm here for you."

I nodded, reached across the table, and wrapped my hand around hers. "I know. And I thank you for being my friend." I paused, thinking about what I'd just said. "You know, I've never thanked you for being my friend before. I guess I'm finally learning true appreciation."

Kristen smiled. "Aww, you're so grown up!"

We both chuckled, knowing we'd cry if we didn't.

"We got into an argument about being together. He called me a scared little girl. He said it because that's how I was acting about being with him. I disagreed. Now we're here." I shrugged and fought back a single tear.

Kristen stood and hugged me again. "I'm so sorry."

I hugged her back.

"But he's not totally wrong."

I glared at her, and she put her hands up defensively.

"Hear me out. You *are* scared to be with him. Why, though, I'll never understand."

"I've told you," I shot back, raising my voice. "I don't have the kind of time to give him the attention he deserves! He's too nice a guy for me! And he's way too hot now, too."

"Now?" Kristen inquired.

"Yeah," I said, calming down. "Did you not know him before?"

"Before when?"

"Ugh, you gotta be so difficult, don't you?" I grinned. "When he showed up the day I shot Sweet, he was round. Like overweight round. His hair was thinning, and his face was perpetually red."

Kristen's mouth dropped open. "What? No way!"

"Yes way. That was when he decided to start working out and caring more about his health and appearance. Just don't tell him I told you about that. He still hopes that none of you remember that he was one of the responding officers." I snickered. "Plus, his doctor told him he'd have to start taking care of himself or he'd be in trouble with his health. I'll take him like this."

"Shit, me too! He's super fine!" She laughed awkwardly. "Sorry. I shouldn't have said that."

"Girl, please. I *know* how hot he is," I said smiling. "I also know how good in bed he is." I winked at her.

"God, I wish I could wink and not look like I'm having a seizure or something," she joked.

We laughed.

"I'll never forget the first time you said that!" I said between giggles. "Man, those were good times."

"Yeah, they were," she agreed. "Okay, now that I know you're better, I guess I'll leave you to it." Kristen stood and placed her glass in the sink.

I stood and walked her to the door. "Thanks for being you."

We hugged.

As she left, she turned and said, "I can't be anyone else. I've tried."

I chuckled and waved before closing and locking the door. I actually did feel much better.

Back in the kitchen, I responded to the rest of the unanswered emails I'd left when Kristen arrived. Then I shut the laptop down and quit for the day. It was almost four, and I didn't have anything left to do anyway.

My mind wandered, forming images of Stu. He now wore his hair in a buzz-cut like Adam Levine did not too long ago. Stu had worked really hard at losing weight too. His body was chiseled nicely: six-pack abs, solid chest and back with amazing definition. He wasn't bulky, just fit. And those blue-gray eyes that sparkled when he looked at me...

My eyes misted, and I shook my head, intent on re-moving the images. I needed to get on with my life. If Stu came back, great. If not, well, I figured I'd get over it and never fall in love again. Which was starting to be an acceptable path. If being in love meant feeling like this all the time, I didn't want anything to do with it. What I did want was something else to do for the time being.

The weather wasn't terrible, so I decided to sit out on the patio and read. I'd neglected the series Brian and I shared a love for long enough. So, I grabbed the hardcover copy of the next in the series that I'd picked up a while ago and set it on the table. Then I poured a glass of water, added a squeeze from the plastic lemon-shaped bottle, and read until the sun set. Even then, I only stopped long enough to feed the cat and order my own dinner.

I'd read to just past the halfway point by the time my dinner arrived. I placed a napkin as a bookmark, and retrieved the food that waited for me at the front door. On the short walk there, I realized how much reading calmed me. Like music did for some animals in studies that I'd read. It had also gotten me focused on something other than Stu. But I hated reading while eating, so I turned on the recorded version of the news so I could listen to the weather forecast.

When I was finished, I went onto the patio to retrieve the book, thinking to read until I fell asleep. I locked the house up and did just that, much to Minion's chagrin.

"Sorry, kid. Cuddle or don't," I told her as I situated myself. I'd accidentally dropped books on her in bed enough to make her weary.

I'd told myself "*one more chapter*" so much, I'd lost track. The last words of the book echoed in my mind. It introduced one character to another in a sort of cliffhanger. The images it evoked were dark, not un-like my own.

I smiled devilishly and closed my eyes.

Seven

A FEW MORE WEEKS had gone by. I'd heard nothing from Stu and had been doing better with going back to who I was. So much so that when Andrew stormed into my office, I laughed. Not because I didn't care—I truly didn't—but because I knew his issue was that Jim was probably being harder on him than anyone else.

"Brit, I can't take it anymore!" His face was flushed.

"Sit," I said, turning back to my computer screen.

Andrew paced in front of my desk, wringing his hands at his sides. "Too much energy."

I snorted and smirked. "Fine, then be pissed off. Not my problem."

"Well fuck you too," he spat.

I clicked my tongue in my mouth, making that noise that moms make when a kid is in trouble. And I kept typing. "I don't think that's what you mean, Andrew. If you did, you'd be here to quit, not bitch. Or you wouldn't be here at all."

He stopped in his tracks. "How did you know that? Did he call you?"

"Nope. I just know the tantrums. You forget I own this agency and have had many conversations that started out this way. Now, sit or don't. But speak now before I lose patience I don't have."

Like a well-trained dog, Andrew sat. He crossed his legs, one ankle resting on top of the other knee. Then he sighed, but didn't say anything.

"Don't stare at me. It's rude. You know how I feel about rude people."

"Just like the good Doctor Lecter," he replied with a sly grin. "Brit, you know how to calm me down. And heat me up."

"Ugh. You're gross. No. Talk to me that way again, and you can find a new job," I said flatly. I turned in my chair to face him. "*And* that will go on your record."

"Whoa!" He raised his hands, palms facing me, and slid back in the chair. "I didn't mean to offend you. I just thought—"

"No, you didn't think. That's the problem. If this is how you learn, so be it." I wasn't angry or offended. I was annoyed. His sleazy attitude would get him nowhere with me; of that he needed to be certain.

He stared at me, and I saw the gears in his mind race. Then he spoke. "I'm sorry, Britney. Truly. Can you forgive me?"

I lied. "Yes. Now, did you want to vent and get some constructive feedback? Or just pitch a fit, hit on me, and leave?"

He stood and bowed a bit. "I think I'll take some time to cool down and try talking to you later."

"Good choice," I said. "Have a good rest of your day." I turned back to my screen.

Andrew had far too much energy to walk out and not look back. Plus, Andrew was a skeeze, the type of guy who'd always look back on the off chance that his charms had somehow worked. Barb had left earlier, not feeling well, so I couldn't even be mad at her for letting him just walk in that way.

The rest of the day was placid. It carried though until I went to bed. What a shame that my only excitement in weeks had been Andrew getting frustrated and trying to come on to me again in the process. I'd have to change that.

I sent a message in the new group text—the one that didn't include Shae.

Ladies night this weekend?

Then I made myself some pasta salad for the evening's dinner. While the pasta cooked, I chopped some bell pepper and cheese. If I could live off cheese and everything else that the doctors said was unhealthy, I would. Including burgers. And that was what I wanted most from ladies' night. Good drinks, great friends, and awesome food.

By the time I'd mixed everything together with some Italian dressing and sat down to watch a movie, my phone had gone off quite a bit. The girls were glad I'd come around and finally wanted to do something. They unanimously agreed that Friday night at The Pub was ideal.

See you then! I replied.

It was good to have something to look forward to. Not that I didn't have anything—I *was* planning to kill Andrew next—but it had been over a month since our last fun night together. I missed it.

I'd put on the next episode of *Dexter*. It was a show I could never tire of. Though I did always stop watching for a time right as season four came to an end. Every time. Without fail. I always picked up some new sliver of something, whether it was information or something I could apply to being a real-life serial killer. The value of fiction in reality was underappreciated.

Before I realized it, season three had ended. I looked at my watch and made a high-pitched noise of surprise. I jumped up to rinse out the bowl I'd eaten from and put food in Minion's bowl before going to bed. It was that late.

I turned the TV in my bedroom on for background noise to fall asleep to and got comfortable. I apparently wasn't tired enough to fall asleep, so after an hour of tossing and turning, I decided to put on a movie I was okay with falling asleep to. That movie was one I'd seen a million times since I was a teenager. It was also one of my favorites. And I didn't care that loving dinosaurs that were on a diet of humans made me look childish.

I pressed the play button and smiled as I heard the music. Then Minion hollered from downstairs, and tore up the stairs and into bed. I laughed and curled up with her.

My phone rang. I rolled over and silenced it. Then turned it to silent so that if it rang again, it wouldn't bother me. I rolled back into the spot I was before, closed my eyes, and fell asleep.

When I woke in the morning, my phone had five text messages, four missed calls, and one voicemail. They were all from Andrew.

I had a feeling that they'd irritate me, so I read and listened before going for my daily jog.

The texts started out nicely, with him apologizing again for his behavior earlier in the day. However, they grew increasingly ignorant, and the voicemail he'd left was the nail in his metaphorical coffin. He wasn't getting an actual coffin.

It didn't matter that he had been drunk and slurring when he left the message. It didn't matter that he'd be calling any minute now to apologize. *He* didn't matter to me anymore, other than my need to keep him around long enough to kill him. The timing wasn't right for me to just stab him now and be done. I had to wait if I didn't want to draw unwanted attention.

I also had to wait out Stu. Had he told anyone? I still didn't know and was beginning to believe that I'd never know. That I'd always be more on my guard than I'd ever been before. I didn't think Stu would ever speak to me again. Not that I could fault him. Killer and cop fall in love. Killer confesses to cop. Then what?

I listened to Andrew's message one last time. I wanted to use it as extra fuel for my jog.

"Just because you pay me doesn't mean you own me…I know what you want, baby…"

He must have been totally hammered to have a full conversation that douchey with a recording. The anger that I felt rising was a combination of things. At Andrew for being slimy, at myself for telling Stu, at Stu for leaving me hanging…

"Ahhh!" I screamed, and Minion cocked her head to the side a little, as if to ask if I wanted to talk about it. I petted her and apologized.

I walked faster than usual to Bayshore Boulevard and even jogged across to the bay side. My earbuds played violent rock and metal music. I felt the beat and let it out.

My feet bounced off the concrete until it was no more. The closer to the base entrance I'd gotten, the less I realized there was no sidewalk. When my feet hit the dirt and sand combination, I slowed to a stop. I was only yards from the gate to MacDill.

"Hmph," I muttered and turned back the way I'd come.

When I got back into my house, I was sweating hard. Jogging on sand wasn't ever my idea of fun, and this trip into it was accidental. My clothes were so stuck to me, I was almost afraid I'd have to cut them off. Luckily, they peeled off, sort of like an orange. The one that the rind seems glued onto and fingers pierce the fruit itself.

My phone rang while I showered, and I tried my best to not wonder if it was Andrew calling again. When I got out, I waited to check my phone until I was almost ready to leave for the office.

I picked up my phone.

It read: 1 Missed Call.

I swiped to unlock the screen, not paying much attention, and opened the voicemail app. I pressed play.

"You fucking asshole."

Eight

His voice was unmistakable. It hadn't been terribly long since the last time I'd heard it, but I'd still almost forgotten what he sounded like.

"I don't know what you expected would happen when you told me about your hobby, Britney."

I gulped, terrified, but I kept listening.

"Gators are dangerous. I can't believe you just hang around them!"

I sighed. Joe Osten was going to give himself another heart attack worrying about me like that. But I'd never heard him speak that way. At least not to me about me. It was kind of scary if I was being honest.

I called him back on my drive into the office, but he didn't answer. So I left him a message.

"Tag, you're it." I began. "Thanks for freaking me out. I really thought you were furious with me, not calling me crazy. Anyway, we should do lunch or something soon. I'm sorry I haven't been talkative lately. Stu and I haven't spoken in…Well, I can tell you in person. Let me know what works for you. Love you."

I ended the call as I pulled into the parking lot. As usual, Barb was already in the office. I smiled, knowing I had truly found myself another great assistant. This one was thanks to my former assistant turned second office manager.

"Good morning, Britney," Barb said as I entered.

"Hey, Barb. How are you?"

"Great, thanks. Do you have a second?"

"Sure," I said, walking to grab my cardigan from the rack. "What's up?"

"Did you mean it when you said I could leave early to look at places with Jim?" She twisted her hands together, obviously nervous.

"Of course I did. Find anything yet?"

She nodded, her face flushing and returning to its normal shade. "Maybe. It's the first place we could agree on to actually want to see in person."

"Congratulations! Just let me know when you're leaving and when you'll be back. You know, within reason," I replied with a smile. I walked back into my office and wished I'd booted up before answering her.

"Thank you, Britney! You're really the best boss. I mean that. Most other bosses weren't as flexible or understanding as you." She coughed a little.

"How are you feeling, anyway?" I asked her.

"Much better. I think it's just nerves, honestly."

"Try smoking weed," I joked. "Or maybe CBD, since I hear it doesn't give you the munchies."

Barb giggled as the phone rang.

I realized I did care about her and her overall well-being. Not as just an employee, but also not too close a friend to invite her out with us. Or out with me alone. I wanted to get to know her more before any of that could happen.

I'd gotten so lost in habit and my own thoughts before realizing it was noon. As if on cue, Barb came to the doorway, shouldering her purse.

"Okay, I should be back around two. We're headed to Carrollwood."

"Carrollwood is a great area! I hope you like it."

"Thanks," Barb said, and checked her watch. "Gotta go or I'll be late. Thanks again, Britney."

"You're—"

The door chime sounded. I giggled. I should have walked her to the door to lock it but didn't. In retrospect, that was a bad idea.

The door chimed again.

"One minute!" I called.

"No worries," Andrew said, sliding into the doorway. He leaned on the door frame and smiled grossly at me. "I came to pick you up for lunch."

"Are you out of your mind?" I was angry this time.

"What?" he asked, faking innocence.

"Get out. After that message you left me last night, just, UGH! GET! OUT!" My face was growing warmer with every word. I hadn't been this angry in a long time.

Andrew backed up slowly, hands up. "I'm sorry, Brit. I was drunk…and…I didn't mean it. I swear! I'm so sorry. Please forgive me?"

"You've asked that twice in as many days. I'm too angry to answer that now. Just get the fuck out of here. Don't come back unless you're invited. Got it?" The heat started to drain from my face, leaving my mind swirling.

"You got it," he said, his voice shaking. He turned and sped out the door so fast the chime barely registered.

"And good riddance," I said to the computer screen.

Barb came back, though at what time I didn't know. I wasn't watching the clock; I'd had emails to respond to. And the lawyer called to advise me that the contract revisions had been sent over to the guy who thought pushing Julie around was a good idea. I was on the phone when she came in.

"Brit! I'm back!" she called from her desk.

I didn't answer her, so she walked into the doorway. She made a face and mouthed the word "oops" then ducked away back to her desk.

"How did it go?" I asked as I placed the handset into its cradle.

"Great! We signed a lease!" Barb's face was lit up as she walked in, stopping just behind a chair in front of my desk.

"That's awesome! Where? When do you move in?" I was genuinely happy for her. Barb was a good person, from what I knew, and she deserved to be happy.

"November first."

I looked at my desk calendar, then back up at her. "That's more than enough notice for me to get you a gift," I said, grinning at her.

"That's really not necessary," she replied, blushing.

"I know, but I want to. It's an occasion that should be marked, even if only in some small way." I wasn't going to suggest she write it on a calendar for the next ten years or anything, but it really was an occasion of note.

Barb smiled. "Yeah, it is kinda special, isn't it? Jim's the first guy I've lived with, aside from family." Then she snapped into action like an internal switch had flipped. "Back to work."

And then I was alone in my office. I smiled thinking about today's events. Even Andrew's creepy visit.

My cell phone rang, bringing me back to the here and now. The screen showed Julie's name.

"Oh shit. How could I have forgotten?" I answered.

"Whoa, Brit. What are you talking about? You okay?" Julie replied.

"Dinner. Like two weeks ago. I wrote it in my planner then forgot. I'm so sorry!"

"Oh, uh…"

"You forgot too?" It was like we'd had our minds wiped by aliens or something.

Julie laughed. "Guess so! Life has been so crazy lately! First, Brian and his anger issues, then Cody's promotion, and this contract situation…That's why I'm calling, actually," she breathed.

"The contract? It's been sent off al—"

"No, Brian. Brian is the reason. Sorry. My mind is finally slowing back down." I heard an uneven smile in her voice.

"Is he okay? Are you okay? What's going on?"

"We're all much better. Dr. Peterson is awesome. Seriously, he's great. Brian likes him a lot too, which is a big deal."

"Glad to hear it. So, lunch? Dinner?"

"Dinner. Tomorrow," she said, though it sounded more like an order.

"You got it. Seven?"

"Yeah. See you then, Brit."

"Jules, before you hang up. Look, don't worry about this contract. You did the right thing, and I'm proud of you for putting your foot down. Don't stress about it, okay?" *I* wasn't worried and she really had acted the way I always knew she could.

"Thank you. That really means a lot to me. I was always afraid to be forceful with clients. Guess I thought they would just walk away from us," she admitted.

"He can go if he wants. Losing him isn't the end of Passing Through."

"I know. I just don't want to be the reason anyone leaves."

"He would be his own reason. Seriously, don't worry. He'll agree to the new terms, or he won't. It's not your fault he's being a dick," I said.

"Shit! APPLESAUCE! I gotta go, Brit. Love you!"

She yelled a little more as she ended the call. I was curious why she kept bringing Applesauce to work if he was being such a pest but decided I'd ask tomorrow night.

I glanced at the clock in the bottom corner of my computer screen and saw that it was somehow almost four. I packed up my things, deciding to just go home for the day.

On my way out, I told Barb to call me if she needed anything. She agreed and thanked me again.

"Barb, really. Stop. I got you." I smiled, turned, and left.

Nine

By the time I walked in the front door, it was around 4:15 p.m. I took my shoes off and went into the kitchen. I hadn't eaten lunch but still wasn't hungry. I figured I was still annoyed or even mad. Sometimes I'd just lose my appetite because of those feelings. It wasn't out of any want to lose weight; that was for sure. I never understood it, but I accepted it.

I poured a glass of water and stared out at the lake. The ducks were on the bank, just hanging out. There were even ducklings, about half a dozen or so. I smiled and walked back into the living room, imagining how soft they would have felt.

I made it to the bottom of the stairs before I realized that leaving my glass of water unattended on the coffee table was a bad idea. I backtracked and picked it up again, deciding to take it upstairs with me. Had I left it on the coffee table, chances were high I'd come back down to Minion drinking from it. Or it would have been knocked over and spilled everywhere. That cat was in a mood lately, and I wasn't playing her games.

There was a lump under the comforter that didn't move when I came in. I giggled as I placed the glass on a shelf in the closet—one she couldn't reach unless I picked her up. She still hadn't moved after I made enough noise to wake the dead.

"Typical cat," I said to her. Then I pulled the comforter up, drawing her ire. I laughed at the look on her tiny face, put the comforter back down, and plucked my glass of water from the shelf.

Back downstairs, I didn't feel like watching movies or anything. So I walked back into the kitchen and placed the glass in the fridge. Then I grabbed my keys and headed out to get some bird seed. I'd read a while ago that bread wasn't good for ducks, and I held no desire to kill them.

I'd never been a typical killer. As a kid, I didn't kill animals, either. Just humans, and even that didn't start until I was a teenager. Maybe it was because humans have the ability to make choices. Or maybe it was because I just wanted to be permanently rid of people. It was never something I tried—or even cared to—figure out.

I pulled into the Lowe's parking lot and shifted into park. I felt like an excited child. All I was getting was bird seed, but something about the thought of feeding the ducks just made me that happy.

There was a bounce in my step as I walked through the store to the section where bird seed was. People gave me sideways looks, but I shook them off in amusement. For the first time in what felt like forever, I was lighthearted. If it only lasted until I left this store, I would be alright with that. Having a little of something enjoyable was better than having none at all.

The smallest bag they had was five pounds. I shrugged and picked one up. With this much food, I could feed the ducks for weeks. And if I really wanted to, I could grab a bird feeder and watch even more birds. But all I really wanted to do was feed the ducks.

I paid for the bag and went home, still feeling pretty good. Traffic didn't faze me much, as I bopped my head listening to '90s pop. I parked in my garage and went inside for a container for the food.

I didn't have anything that would fit the entirety of the bag, and I wasn't looking for that. Just something small, a few quarts or something. I had plastic containers for leftovers, so I grabbed the biggest one I had. Then I opened the bag and poured some in. I could have scooped it out, but that would've meant the whole top would need to be closed afterward. Doing it this way, I would only need to close a corner.

I went back out and to the lakeside. The ducks quacked at each other and scrambled to get away from me. I smiled and threw a handful of feed their way. One of the ducklings noticed what it was and waddled over. The rest followed. I watched as I sat on the nearby bench.

In less than two minutes, the group had finished and looked over at me. I threw more onto the grass not far from my feet, and they came over. Soon, I was surrounded by happily chattering ducks and ducklings. My heart felt full, and I was just as happy as they were.

When the food I brought ran out, I stood to go back home. The ducks quacked at me and followed for a bit. I was afraid they'd follow me to my door. But they stopped right before the corner of my patio. They clearly had limits. Not that I could blame them; being around humans was less than preferable.

The sun had dropped to a position where it blinded me as I came around the side. I shielded my eyes as best as I could. For some reason, I hadn't expected it. The position of the sun was normal for the time of year it was. Maybe I just wasn't used to being outside at this time of day. Not that it was terribly concerning since I was walking inside anyway.

Minion sat on the stairs, about halfway down, and stared at me. Too much time had passed since I'd woken her up, so I figured she was just pissy and went on my way.

I dropped the container into the sink and turned the faucet on. Minion hollered at me from the doorway, causing me to scald my hand under too-hot water. I turned the handle toward the wall, making it a little cooler.

"Thanks, M," I said to her as I added soap to the sponge.

By the time I'd washed and dried the container, Minion was seated on a chair at the table. I laughed when I saw her. Then I pulled my glass of water from the fridge. Minion perked up when she saw it.

"No. You have your own," I told her as I walked out to the living room.

As I sat on the couch, I picked up the book I'd left on the coffee table. I knew I would have to be halfway through this one before seeing Brian tomorrow night. Our personal book club would be discussing it and the one prior, of that I was positive. I was already behind on the series, and annoyed that life had gotten in the way. I opened it and started reading.

I felt satisfied with the line I'd read last and placed a tissue as a bookmark. I'd left the only one I had upstairs, inside the last one I read.

I grabbed my phone and went into the kitchen, then snatched up the small bit of paper I'd left on the counter. I was hungry and intended to only pick up the essentials from the small list I'd previously written out and ignored. I glanced at it on my way out the door. Pasta and a few other things were written, but that was it. Was there something wrong with me that I was forgetting even the smallest of things? I shrugged it away and climbed into my Jeep.

Publix was always busy around now; 7 p.m. on a weeknight seemed to be when most people around here shopped. I usually went to Publix around 8 a.m. on Saturdays. Most of the only other people in the store were employees, so it made getting in and out a breeze. Being here now, however, made me want to look further into having groceries delivered. It would also save me from forgetting that I'd even written out a list.

I grabbed a basket from the stack inside the door and made a beeline for the pasta aisle. Or maybe it was more like skiing a slalom course. People were dispersed throughout the store in a weird con-nect-the-dots pattern. Some simply stood in place, not doing much of anything.

The pasta aisle was more cluttered with bodies than I was used to. Again I had to remind myself that it wasn't my normal shopping trip and took a deep breath. I picked up a few boxes of penne, fettuccine, and rigatoni. Though I usually made an olive oil, but-ter, and garlic sauce, I plucked a jar of roasted red pepper sauce off the shelf and placed it in my basket. Satisfied there would be enough to last a minimum of a few weeks, I darted to the wine section.

Six bottles would be too heavy to carry right now, so I picked up two. Total Wine also had a great se-lection—and was an excuse to get out—so I decided going there when I needed more wasn't such a bad idea. Just outside of the wine area was the deli and cheese items that were on my list. I snagged a few of my go-tos and walked to the express checkout.

While I waited, I counted and recounted how many items I had. It always pissed me off me when some-one had more than the amount stated on the sign. And *sometimes* I tried hard not to be a hypocrite.

The cashier was friendly and young. I'd be lying if I didn't admit that giving her my card crossed my mind. But they were in the center console of my Jeep. So I asked her for a pen and wrote my info on the back of the receipt she'd handed me.

"If you're interested…I think I can get you better pay than here," I said and winked.

It was probably bad taste to solicit without a conversation leading up to giving her the info, but she thanked me and smiled.

Back home, I was again greeted by a scream. This time, it was for a reason—it was past feeding time. So I fed Minion then emptied the grocery bags. I had all but the box I planned to open put away when I heard a ruckus outside. I peeked out the window in the kitchen to see the fluffy ducklings chatting furiously. The bigger ducks pecked at the grass. I knew feeding them could cause a problem. Not just by making them dependent or causing them to hang out here all the time, but by annoying the neighbors too. So I ignored the squeaks and chirps and went about making my dinner. I had to try my best to not get into any more tussles with the easily offended/annoyed/crotchety neighbors.

"I'd love to keep feeding them, but ugh. Stupid neighbors will bitch. And for what? Ducks want to be fed. Big fucking deal. Would they bitch about a human wanting to be fed?"

I was talking to myself again. I had too many thoughts in my head that fought for space, and some needed to come out somehow. This was how that happened. I didn't have Stu to lean on now. Maybe I could have called one of the girls, but for what? To vent for three seconds and hang up? That could wait until the neighbors voiced a problem. That was always when I needed to blow off some steam. They used to bitch about damned near everything. Then I shot Sweet.

When my dinner was finished cooking, I sat on the patio to eat it. It was more humid out than it had been when I went to the store, which told me that rain might be on the way. This was Florida, after all, and this type of weather was fairly common.

Thunder sounded, and the sky grew dark in a hurry. I smiled, eager for the relaxing sound of rain. As I ate, the rain started and then fell harder. The idea of watching a favorite scary movie while it rained flashed into my mind. It was enticing enough that when I finished eating, I rinsed the dishes and did just that until I fell asleep on the couch.

Ten

IT WAS DARK WHEN I opened my eyes. Confusion slammed my brain. I turned my left wrist and looked at my watch. It was 3 a.m., and I was still on the couch. I rubbed my eyes as I sat up more. The only light came from the screen saver on the Roku stick I streamed with. I stood and went upstairs, changed, and crawled in bed.

At 6 a.m., I woke to gloom and more rain. Since I wouldn't be going for a jog in this, I rolled over and slept another hour. I didn't feel very rested though. It was as though the 3 a.m. episode had sucked the life out of me for the day. Then I remembered caffeinated things existed and felt mildly better. I had a dinner date tonight I didn't want to miss.

I got to the office a little after nine; there had been a fender bender holding up traffic near my house. As usual, Barb was inside. When I walked in, I noticed she looked as tired as I felt.

"Morning, Barb. You okay? You look beat," I commented, concerned.

"Yeah. I guess. We were up late last night," she responded, not looking up from her cup of coffee.

I set my purse on my desk and came back out, pulling a chair over to Barb's desk and sat.

"Look at me. What's going on?"

"Jim doesn't trust that Andrew guy you sent him, and we fought about it for a little bit until he realized it sounded like he was taking out his anger and frustration on me." She sniffed and continued, "I cried for hours. And I'm not normally one to take things like this personally. I don't know why I did this time. Jim feels terrible about it and so do I. I-I just don't get it, Brit. Why did I take this so hard?"

I put my hand on her arm and squeezed. "You're under a lot of stress right now. Don't be mad at yourself or Jim. Stress makes a person extra sensitive. Believe me, I go through it too. Why do you think I jog so much? Anyway, what do you say we order some Starbucks—extra shot—and something to eat? My treat. Something tells me we could both use it." I smiled, choosing not to acknowledge the bit about Andrew. He'd be gone soon enough. It bothered me to see her so upset and distraught. She was really growing on me.

Barb drank the remainder of the coffee in her cup and smiled back at me. "I'd like that."

"Good. What do you want?" I asked as I opened the app on my phone.

Barb told me and I added it to my "bag," along with my drink and croissant order. Then I booted my computer and left to go pick up our lattes. Barb offered to make the run, but I wasn't having it. The girl needed to stop beating herself up. Plus, I was afraid that if anything got messed up, she'd totally lose it.

When I got back, Barb looked happier than she had when I left. She was also on the phone. I took her drink out of the carrier and set it on the top part of her desk along with her sandwich. She smiled and mouthed the words "thank you" in between answering questions. I smiled back and continued to my office.

At my desk, I started to work and threw back my triple-shot peppermint mocha like it was water after a foot race. I sighed and tried to push the nagging thoughts of *never-ending day* and *slower than molasses in January* out of my head. That only lasted so long.

Lunchtime came, and Barb and I were dragging ass again. If we hadn't been so tired, we'd probably have found it amusing. Though amused was something neither one of us was close to.

"Hey, Barb? Got any tricks to get happy? I've got dinner at Julie's tonight, and I don't want to be a grumpy bitch." I half-giggled.

Barb smiled. "Not really. I'm beat too. Maybe just focus on the happiness you feel when you're at her house?" She shrugged and went back to the kitchen after locking the front door.

Hm. Sounds like she's got a good idea there. So, I gave it a shot. I closed my eyes and concentrated on seeing Brian's smiling face and jokes and good food with good people. It seemed to help for the time being. *If I need to, I'll do it again and again.*

When Barb returned from her break, I took mine. But not the full hour and definitely not to eat. It was too late in the day. Granted, I could eat damned near any time. But I didn't want to chance it and not be hungry for dinner.

I picked up my cell phone and texted Julie.

Still on for tonight?

The phone on my desk rang.

"Yes, goofy-ass," Julie said.

I snickered. "Good. Seeing how we both forgot last time, I figured it would be good to make sure."

"Bring wine. And good conversation."

"You got it," I replied.

The line went dead. Smiling, I shook my head and hung up.

I ran to the gas station across the street for energy drinks and came back chugging one, with more in a bag on my forearm.

Barb looked shocked, but she understood all too well.

Three energy drinks later, it was time to leave for the day. Barb talked to me from her desk as she shut down for the night.

"I am so glad this day is over! I'm going home and straight to bed," she said with a giggle.

"You and me both! But I'm sure I'll be wide awake when I get home from Julie's." The sad part was that I was right. It always seemed to work out that I'd be exhausted going somewhere but when it came time to settle down and actually go to sleep…

We walked out together, and I locked up while Barb got in her car and left.

Per Julie's request for wine, I stopped at Publix and grabbed some on the way to her house.

When she answered the door, I held up two bottles—one in either hand. She squealed, took one, then wrapped me in a hug so tight I thought my eyes would pop out of my skull.

"I missed you too!" I said happily.

"Come on, dinner's almost done." She stood back and let me in. Brian was on the couch reading, and Cody was calling Julie from the kitchen. I ran to hug Brian as I followed Julie.

I put the bottle I was still carrying into the fridge then opened the one Julie had set on the counter. Cody was having a bit of a fight with the cast iron skillet on the stove a few feet away from me. So I poured a glass and exchanged it for the tongs in his hand.

"Scooch," I said, waving him away. "And I need a pot holder."

Cody scrambled to hand me one, sipped from his glass, then poured for me and Julie. He watched my hands intently as I worked the steaks.

"First time with the cast iron," he admitted sheepishly. "I already added butter and garlic, and a little olive oil. I did that right, right?"

"Yeah," I giggled and put the pot holder on the handle, "but the trick is to flip them every two or three minutes to desired doneness. Like me—I like medium-rare, so mine is done." I nodded for him to grab me a plate to put it on. He held one out, and I set the steak on it.

"Let it rest. Want me to keep cooking or you want the tongs back?"

Cody held out his hand, and I gladly handed the tongs back. Then Julie and I clinked glasses and sipped. Brian came in to see what we were doing.

"Hey, pal," Cody said to him. "You missed it. Aunt Brit was giving me a cooking lesson!"

We all chuckled, and Brian just smiled. "Well then. Aunt Brit, I guess we'll have to wait until after dinner to talk books."

I smirked at him. "Damned straight! I've spent the better part of the past three days trying to catch up for tonight."

Brian high-fived me and carried two plates out to the dining room. I mimicked him and followed.

By the time Cody was finished cooking, Brian and Julie and I had the table set. Julie grabbed the second bottle of wine since the first was almost empty, and we all sat down to eat.

Julie and Brian told me how much they liked Dr. Ben Peterson, Brian's therapist and my friend/therapist. They talked animatedly about friends Brian was making in school and about Applesauce, who was currently locked out back and barking like mad.

"Won't your neighbors complain?" I asked, sipping my wine.

Cody shrugged. "Probably not. And if they do, I'll complain about their screaming children."

I chuckled. "That bad?"

Julie emphatically shook her head. "I've been taking Applesauce to the office with me so Cody can work from home and be here for Brian when he gets off the bus." She sipped her wine. "Well, only on the days Brian goes to see Ben. We don't trust him enough to leave him home. Applesauce, I mean." Her face flushed with embarrassment.

"Yeah, and those goddamned kids just screech and scream all afternoon," Cody grumbled as he ate. "Full-day kindergarten doesn't seem to be an option over there."

I nodded sympathetically and ate my steak. "Compliments to the chef." I raised my glass to Cody. "Good work!"

Everyone giggled at my half joke, and we finished our dinner so fast it was surprising no one choked. Even Julie, who had requested the wine, ignored her glass in favor of eating. It was like everyone was breaking a fast. I knew about that kind of thing, having grown up in a family that wasn't religious, but on the truly holy holidays, we sort of observed them. Mainly with good food and family and friends. And the once-a-year fast got us all, every year.

I chewed my last bite and smiled. "Cody, that really was great. The butter-to-garlic ratio was superb." I chef kissed him, and Julie laughed. Brian looked at me impatiently.

Julie caught it and stood, plate in hand. "Let's clear the table so you two can have book talk."

I grinned. "You mean geek talk." Then I took Brian's plate and mine into the kitchen. Brian followed with more plates, and Cody brought up the rear.

"Dish train is in the station," I joked. Julie rolled her eyes at me as she loaded the dishwasher. Brian took my hand and dragged me to the back door.

"Whoa, Nelly! Hang on. The dog's out there. I really don't feel like having him be all over me. Will Jules get mad if we let him in without asking?"

Brian shrugged. "Uh…" Then he called to Julie. "Hey, Julie, can Applesauce come in?"

"Yeah. It's his dinnertime anyway."

He slid the door open and Applesauce jumped on me in his customary greeting. I petted him and told him to go eat. It wasn't until he heard food being poured into his stainless-steel bowl that he realized it was time for him to eat.

Brian was already standing outside, hand on the door handle, waiting for me. He stepped back, allowing me passage.

"Thank you, good sir." I curtsied and he laughed.

"Okay, what book are you on? I don't want to give you spoilers or ruin anything for you." He talked as we walked the few feet to the table.

"Well, I finished the one where they all died and came back in other bodies. I'm halfway through the one after it."

He nodded his acceptance.

"But first, can we talk a little about how you're doing? Seriously. Not just that you like Ben and he's helpful. How are you *feeling*? How is Brian?" I smiled and put a hand on his shoulder.

He half smiled and looked at the table for a few moments. Then he spoke.

"I'm a lot better. He's teaching me how to process my anger and frustration in better ways. I tried journaling, but I don't like it very much. What I do like—and what works—is visualization. I close my eyes and go to my happy place. When I'm there, I focus on the smells, sounds, sights…that kind of thing. And I also focus on my breathing. I know it sounds like a bunch of bullshit. It really does work." He looked up at me as he said that.

"I believe you, Bri. And I'll never judge you. I love you no matter what." I leaned over and kissed him on the cheek. "Now, back to being geeks."

He smiled, and we got into a great, sometimes heated discussion. We talked about where I saw my current read going and what I hoped for the rest of the series. Brian's views weren't the same, and that was my favorite part. We could talk about these books and disagree thoughtfully. That gave me hope for having more "adult" conversations with him.

The light above our heads came on, and Julie poked her head out of the door. "Hey, you two. Want dessert?"

Brian lit up and I nodded.

Inside, Julie had already set out Danish and coffee. My mouth watered at the sight of the Danish and I sat down.

"Are you a mind reader?" I asked her. "It's been a long twenty-four hours, and I could use the boost to drive home."

Julie's mouth was full of Danish, so she simply smiled and raised her mug in a toast. I raised mine simultaneously with Cody and Brian. I sipped and eyed Brian while he sipped whatever was in his.

"Whatcha got in there?" I asked him.

"Irish coffee," he responded with a wink.

I nodded. "Ah. So Irish Cream creamer in decaf. Got it."

"Thanks, Aunt Brit. Make me look like a dork, why don't you?" He poked back at me.

As we were finishing our dessert and coffee, my phone rang. I ignored it. It rang again.

"Ugh, this best be important," I grumbled as I fished through my purse to stop it from ringing.

I looked at the screen and dropped my phone on the table.

Eleven

THE NAME ON THE screen was Andrew York.

I was less than amused when I answered.

"What?"

"Well, that's not a proper greeting," he sneered.

"What do you want, Andrew?"

"Nope, still not proper," he replied.

"If you don't tell me what you want, I'm hanging up."

He sighed. "Okay, fine. I wanted to let you know that I don't think Jim wants to keep me around, even temporarily."

Neither one of us does. We'll both get our wish soon enough, I heard that little voice in my head say.

"Well, he hasn't said anything to me. Do you want me to keep an eye out for another placement?" I knew Jim was just being hard on him to test him, but I also knew Jim didn't trust him. What I didn't know was why. I made a mental note to call Jim tomorrow and find out what was going on.

"No. I just thought you should know, is all." His voice held that tinge of playfulness it had when he was trying to seduce me.

"Andrew, it's after five. Therefore not business hours. Please call back then. And stop calling my personal cell phone to discuss business. You are my employee, and you calling me like this is inappropriate. Got it? Cool. Have a great night!"

I hung up and edited the contact name in my phone to read Do Not Answer - Andrew York. He wouldn't be the first person I'd done that to. And definitely not the last.

I dropped the phone back into my purse and looked at everyone seated around me. They all wore amused expressions, particularly Julie.

"That louse still wants to get in your pants?" She laughed at her own question.

Cody and I flashed each other looks, mouthing "louse?" Brian, however, didn't mouth it.

"Louse? Really? Are we in a musical now? Or is it the fifteen hundreds and this word is in common usage?" Then he burst into fits of laughter, earning him a glare from Julie. Cody and I had to turn away, our eyes watering from holding in our giggles.

"You two are encouraging this! You're so grounded, all three!" Julie flushed and laughed. "I guess I do sound old, now that I think about it."

"You guess?" Cody asked.

We all laughed again, though I don't think Brian had ever stopped. Julie stood, still giggling, and gathered napkins and plates. I helped and followed her back to the kitchen. We shared a few more giggles at her expense before walking back into the living room. Then I picked up my purse and said my good-nights.

The drive home was surprisingly quick, and when I got there the house was dark. I'd forgotten to leave lights on, which created a bit of a challenge. I had no gun on me either, just a small flip knife in my purse. I was sure it wasn't sharp enough to do much damage to even packing tape, but I was also no stranger to break-ins. My other concern was tripping over or stepping on the cat.

I hopped out of the Jeep and turned the flashlight on my phone on before unlocking the door. I did my best to illuminate the room and behind the door while holding the knife and locking the door at the same time. It was awkward, at best. But then I found my way upstairs and pulled the Glock from the safe before checking the rest of the house. Sure, it was a paranoid move, but I needed to be sure the house was clear.

When I was, I resolved to research the best way to purse carry—not that I was even a fan of that particular idea, but something had to give. I'd been broken into, stalked, and everything else. I needed to start carrying again outside of the house—wondering why I'd stopped would just be useless. Which also meant opening up to new carry options. That was the easier part. The research on purse carry, however, would be weeks of nausea and headaches.

I could have gotten an alarm, too, but after Sweet, I didn't feel the desire. Had I had one then, he could have set the alarm off and claimed to be the responding officer. Life would be much different now, had that been the situation. But now that Andrew was back around and being extra slimy, I wouldn't put it past him to find a way in here. He wouldn't steal anything. More like he'd be waiting on my bed for me. Naked. I'd have to burn the sheets after.

I fed the cat and watched some TV in bed before dozing off.

In the morning, I placed a coffee pick-up order the same as the day before as a surprise for Barb. The drive-thru line was always horrendous, and I wasn't a fan of lattes that got cold. I parked and went inside. There was a designated space for pick-ups, and I found the order easily.

When I got to the office, Barb wasn't there. I couldn't remember if she told me she'd be late or not. I placed the carrier on the ground so I could open the door, then picked it up and went inside. Inside was a little chilly, so I put Barb's drink in the microwave in an attempt to keep it warm for her.

My computer booted up and I happily sipped my latte and picked at the croissant on my desk. It asked for the password and I entered it. The computer dinged at me, displaying "The PIN entered is incorrect." I entered it again and got the same response. It was then that I looked at my keyboard to see numbers on the 10-key switched around.

"Who could have been here?" I asked myself aloud.

As if to answer, my phone rang. I answered and heard cackling on the other end.

"Dammit, Julie!" I started giggling.

"Sorry, I'm in a mood today. Then again, maybe that was payback for the old-person jokes. Thanks for coming over last night. Brian misses you already," she said.

"Aww, I miss him too. Thanks for having me! It was way overdue. Let's not wait so long next time, huh?"

"You got it. Look, what's-his-name asshole emailed. He's trying to renegotiate the contract through me."

"Ugh. Okay. Call the lawyer and let him know please. For me to tell him won't matter; he'll still want to talk to you." I sighed. "I'm sorry he's being like this. Want to just cut ties if we can?"

"I don't know. What do you think? It's *your* company," she replied.

"Yeah, but he's trying to take advantage of *your* good nature," I shot back.

"Ugh, fine. I am mad, but I'm trying not to think about it. You went the correct route by getting the lawyers involved in the first place. This guy's a douche nozzle, and I refuse to lose money—and my temper—over him. Are you really okay with losing him? I mean, he does bring in a considerable amount of money."

"I'm sure. I looked at the books, and we actually don't make that much profit. We could make more by bringing on another local business…There's one in particular…" I shuffled through some papers in my inbox on my desk, "Hang on…I'll find it." Then the phone slid from between my ear and shoulder. "Shit!"

I found the paper shortly after, but Julie had hung up by the time I retrieved the dropped phone. I dialed her back. Busy. So I sent her an email with the name and other information contained on the printed-out contact form from the Passing Through website. All of those emails were routed to Barb's email, and she printed them for me to go over because I'm old school like that. This one was in the area of Julie's office, so I figured she could handle it. It was a retirement home on Bearss Avenue. I'd talked to the manager a few times at events a colleague had invited me to but nothing truly substantial.

My phone rang again.

"Jules, he's all yours. Super nice guy. Promise."

"Uh, is this Passing Through Temp Agency?" the man asked.

"Oh wow. I'm so sorry! I was expecting someone else. May I help you?"

"This is Jim. Is this Britney?"

"Hey, Jim! I was going to call you after I talked to Julie. What's going on with you and Andrew?"

"That's exactly why I'm calling. He's…weird. I can't really explain it, but it's like something inside his brain is…well, broken."

I cackled then cleared my throat. "Excuse that. Yes, he is strange. I've known him a long time. You can trust him; I know that for sure. At least with job-related matters and tasks. He can be creepy and slimy, but that's only because he thinks he's God's gift to women."

"Is that what it is? I knew he was arrogant about something, but I never heard anything from either of the women here about him. Should I be worried?"

"No. He's not that stupid. Just tell him he needs to buck up. Or I can pull him if you'd like."

"No, no, I need a body, and he *does* do good work. Okay, I'll have a chat with him and see what happens. I'd hate to lose him because he's cocky. When I say he does good work, I should be clearer. I'm impressed. He works like someone who's been in accounting for twenty years. It would be sad to let him go because he can't get over himself. Thanks, Britney. I'll talk to him later. May I ask, would you be upset if I chose not to keep him?"

I smiled. "Absolutely not, Jim. I know Andrew can be a handful. I wouldn't have sent him over if I weren't confident that you could set him straight."

"Thanks for the kind words. They mean a lot. You know, Barb really likes you. And thanks for being cool about us going apartment hunting during work hours."

"No problem. I see it this way: If Barb isn't happy at home, then she'll probably do poor work or have bad interactions with clients. Believe me, I've had too much experience with that kind of thing. I'm really happy for the two of you."

"Thank you, Britney. Really. For everything. I've gotta go. Talk soon," Jim replied.

"Any time," I said. "Have a good one."

"You too." He hung up. I smiled. My good deed for the year had been done. Not that I kept track, but I would consider promoting blossoming love between two people I hardly knew a good deed large enough to cover an extended period of time. Encouraging Julie and Cody had been different—I'd known Julie a few years, and we were fairly close.

The door chimed while I was deep in my inbox.

"It's just me. Sorry I'm late. There was a fire alarm in my building at 2 a.m., and I had a hard time getting back to sleep. Then I missed my alarm.," Barb called to me.

"No worries! Glad you're okay. Oh! There's a latte for you in the microwave," I replied.

"Where?"

"The microwave. That's where I put it hoping to keep it warm-ish." I didn't look away as I continued to send responses.

"Oh! Thanks!" The clacking of her shoes faded in the hallway and came back. Neither of us said another word for a while.

Hours went by before Julie replied to the email I'd sent about a potential new client.

Brit,

Talked to him. Meeting tomorrow. Keep you posted.

Jules

I didn't bother to reply, knowing she'd gotten a read receipt from the email program. Then I glanced at the clock. Barb's lunch time. I listened harder for any noises coming from the reception area. Keys on a keyboard clacked away madly.

"Barb, go to lunch," I called.

"Brought it with me. Going to the kitchen to eat in a minute," she replied.

I clacked some more myself, and she poked her head in. "Joining me?"

"Thanks. Maybe tomorrow. I'm just gonna leave like an hour or so early today."

Barb made an exaggerated sad face. "Okay." Then she was gone.

I looked up the number for our alarm system guy and left him a message asking for him to call me back. I was thinking of maybe setting up an appointment for him to meet me at the house. Or just some over-the-phone guidance on systems. Whichever he'd be able to provide.

He called back a few minutes later and we set the appointment for that afternoon. From that point on, the afternoon dragged.

I think I just wanted to go home and take a nap or something. I wasn't tired; I just couldn't focus.

Three-thirty finally rolled around, and I jumped out of my seat, shutting down for the night. It had been a while since I was this excited to go home for what may have ultimately been a bullshit reason.

On the drive there, I wondered why—and if—I truly wanted an alarm system. I was sure cameras would be a good idea, but wasn't entirely sold on them for a variety of reasons.

I got home with enough time to change my shoes as Jon pulled up to my house. He got out of his truck and waved. I met him at the end of the driveway and we briefly discussed that he'd take a walk around, inside and out, then come up with a few different options and email them to me. He was done and gone in less than forty-five minutes.

I lay down on the couch, turned a movie on, and passed out.

Twelve

I woke to my cell phone ringing. The name on the screen didn't register in my brain before I answered.

"Hello?" My voice cracked.

There was a long pause. "Hi, Brit."

I must have thought I was dreaming because I kept talking. "Are you coming over? I miss you."

Again he paused. "I can. Do you really want me to?"

"Yes."

"Okay, we can talk about this face to face. That's probably best anyway." He terminated the call.

I knew it was Stu on the other end of that call. What I didn't know was how my brain failed me so hard at such a crucial moment. He was on his way here, and I'd been woken up by his call. There was still crusted drool at the corners of my mouth, for fuck's sake.

I ran upstairs to rinse from the nose down. As I dabbed dry, I spoke into the mirror. "What am I doing? Is he really coming over? Why am I freaking out?"

I'd barely gotten the words out when the doorknob on the front door jiggled, followed by the doorbell.

Is he really here? Ohmigod. He's here. It's been...

How long *had* it been? I shook my head and slinked down the stairs. At the bottom, I paused, suddenly unsure of reality. Was I dreaming?

The bell sounded, followed by knocking, and his voice. "Brit, you here?"

I took a deep breath and steadied myself, then opened the door.

He smiled that crooked smile at me. My heart thumped so hard I thought it would come out of my chest. His blue-gray eyes sparkled. "You gonna let me in?"

"Oh, sorry. I'm still asleep," I said, stepping back from the doorway.

Stu entered and hugged me. We danced a bit—moving our arms around and going in for it—trying to figure out the right way to do this. It was awkward. After all, I *had* told him I was a killer. Yet here he was, standing in front of me. I closed the door and eyed him suspiciously.

"Sweet was right all along. Now what?" I asked snidely, folding my arms across my chest.

"Why the hostility? Brit, can we—can we sit down?" He moved toward the couch as he asked.

This had to be some form of entrapment or something. There was no way he was here for any other reason than to arrest me. Right? I knew I couldn't have it both ways. Either I stopped killing people and maybe we could be together, or he used our intimate knowledge of each other to arrest me.

He sat on the couch and patted the cushion next to him. "Please, sit. I swear I'm not here to lock you up."

I stood there like an indignant child, even swaying a bit. "Prove it. Show me you're not wearing a wire."

He stood and pulled his shirt up. I'd nearly forgotten how well defined his stomach and lower back were. He turned slowly, making sure I saw there was nothing taped to him. Then he sat back down and patted the cushion again.

I sighed heavily and walked over. Arms still crossed, I stood there and stared at him. "Why are you here?"

He looked hurt yet happy to see me. "To talk. Please. Sit with me."

I sat, keeping my distance. We looked at each other for a minute then he found my eyes—the soul I didn't think I had—and looked at it. I mean, he *really* looked at it. I felt his gaze penetrate my skin and wrap my insides in that kind of rom-com reunion hug. The one where the girl thinks they'll never be together, and the guy shows up and holds her until the sun rises. And the passion can be felt through the screen. *That* kind of hug. I melted into the back of the couch.

Stu's eyes smiled at me; his mouth twitched. Yet I still felt the need to be defensive. Like he wasn't as in love with me as I was with him. His face said it all; he didn't need to speak. But I wanted to hear it.

"Brit..." He looked down and grabbed my hand, holding it, playing with my fingers. Then he looked up. Our eyes locked. I felt like I'd burst into tears at any second. "Brit, I love you. I spent a lot of time thinking about what to do and what's right. What's right is us being together. What's right is that I love you. What's right is us. Right here, right now. *We* are right."

He stopped to catch his breath.

My heart stopped waiting for the inevitable blow that would shatter what heart I had.

"But nothing's gonna stop us. I'm still going to be a cop. You'll still be a killer. And I'll be damned if I'm gonna let the love of my life die for who she is." Whatever barrier he'd managed to hold inside his tear ducts broke. My eye dams did, too.

I flung my arms around him. "You mean it? You want to be with me?"

"Yes! I'll shout it from the rooftops, Brit. I love you. And I'll do whatever I have to to make sure we stay together."

I pulled back, tears leaving ribbons of color down my face. "Even if it means losing your job?"

"Even if it means losing my job. Britney Cage, I *love* you." He kissed me. It was the most passionate kiss we'd shared yet. My nerve endings exploded like tiny fireworks, even the ones in my brain popped and fizzled and sang.

I laid my head on his chest for a long time after that kiss, fighting to hold on to reality. I was convinced it was a dream. One of those dreams that felt so real, and then you woke up to bleakness and despair.

Then I opened my eyes. My head was still on Stu's chest. I smiled.

"I know now isn't such a great time, but why do you spell your name S-T-U when you spell Stewart with and e and a w?"

He laughed, and caressed my face, sliding a bit of stray hair behind my ear. "Because if I spell it the other way, it looks like I'm a food."

I laughed. "Never thought of it that way." I kept my face against his chest and stayed silent. I stroked his chest and stomach. I needed to feel that his body next to mine was still real. I hadn't been getting as much sleep as I should have and had drunk enough since he last left to be hallucinating from withdrawal.

Stu put his hands on my shoulders and sat me up, then sat up himself. He rubbed my shoulders a minute before standing. He held my hands with his the whole time. When he stood, he held my arms out, encouraging me to stand with him. I did. He led me upstairs to my bed, where I changed into pajamas and crawled under the covers. Stu only took off his shoes and belt and joined me. I laid my head on his chest staring at the ceiling. Stu stroked my hair. Neither one of us slept that night as we enjoyed the simple fact that we were together. Something we'd try not to take for granted ever again.

Thirteen

IT WAS JUST AFTER 9 a.m. that I called Barb at the office to let her know I wouldn't be in. She asked if I was alright, and I assured her I was.

The truth was I hadn't slept a wink the night before, owing to the fact that I still didn't trust reality. Yet here he was, still next to me. After all I'd done and confessed to. Stu Jones was back. And he wanted to be here as long as I'd have him.

My hand still on his chest, I sat up and looked at him.

"What's up?" he asked.

"This is so unbelievable," I said. "How can you justify our being together and still be a cop?"

"John Wayne Gacy's family had no idea there were decomposing bodies under their feet, and they loved him anyway," Stu said.

"They had no idea. Or they were in denial. This isn't the same." I stopped myself, unsure of what I was trying to say.

Stu sat up and kissed my cheek. "Love makes people do crazy things. I'm of sound mind and have been;

I'm not playing the insanity card here. Honestly, I'm not 100 percent sure how to say it. I just feel it deep into my core. That somehow I can help guide you to not get caught while maintaining ignorance at work. Hell, I'd cover things up if that's what I have to do to keep you safe."

I sat there in shock. I loved this man with all of my being, but it was such an incredible thing. I began to wonder whose moral compass was more broken. *A cop dating a killer and playing stupid to the department.* The thoughts suddenly streamed from my mouth.

"Who would believe that?"

"Brit, leave that to me," he said softly and smiled. "Let's get some sleep, huh?"

I smiled back, still in a state of disbelief, and lay down again. Stu wrapped an arm around me and soon I was asleep.

When I woke up, the sky was purple, pink, and an orange-yellow as the sun disappeared over the horizon. I didn't feel an arm on me and sighed.

"I knew it wasn't real," I said, rolling over. I didn't want to see the empty pillow next to me, but needed to know it was all a dream.

He was there. Asleep.

I almost squealed from pure joy but clapped my hand over my mouth instead. I watched him for a while before he woke up, eyes opening slowly as a smile spread across his lips.

"You're cute when you're creepy," he said.

Protesting would have been stupid; I was absolutely not trying to be creepy. But watching anyone sleep—aside from a baby—*was* creepy. I giggled and kissed his cheek. Then pushed the covers off and stood up.

As I brushed my teeth, Stu came in. "Hungry?"

I nodded and tried to speak, but I spit toothpaste everywhere instead.

Stu laughed.

I wanted to but was afraid I'd choke on my toothbrush. After I rinsed, I spoke. "Yeah. Want to order delivery?"

"Well, I was thinking to run home and brush my teeth and change first."

I made a noise that sounded like "psssh" and pulled a brand new toothbrush from a drawer. Stu smirked as I handed it to him.

"You got a change of clothes for me too?" he asked, opening the package and putting toothpaste on it.

My face twisted into a frown. "No. But there's plenty of room in the closet if you want to keep a spare outfit here." I didn't want more of his clothes than necessary here; I guessed I was waiting for the ship to run aground.

Stu paused his brushing and grinned. Toothpaste dribbled down his chin, and I burst into laughter. He may have been an adult, but he was also a big kid. I adored that about him.

I skimmed my fingertips up and down his back as he bent over to rinse. Goosebumps littered his skin.

He straightened and wrapped his arms around my waist, kissing me hard. I melted like butter.

He pulled away and studied my face. "You okay?"

"Duh."

Stu giggled and released me. "I'll believe that when you can stand up straight."

I felt myself swaying, and my face flushed.

"Bah," I waved, "I'm fine."

I walked on wobbly legs to the top of the stairs. I felt much less shaky by the time my foot touched the entry floor downstairs. Stu followed, every now and then touching my arm to make sure I was okay.

From the couch, a curled-up Minion eyed us, her head upside-down. Stu petted her as I walked into the kitchen and took her food out of the pantry. She must have been hungry because when her food hit the inside of her bowl, she was suddenly at my feet.

"You've been replaced by food," I joked to Stu.

"She'll come back; they always do." He chuckled.

"Do they now?" I raised an eyebrow.

Stu wrapped his arms around me as I turned away from the pantry and kissed me. "No. But it does seem that *I* come back."

I kissed him and pulled away. "I'm hungry too. What are we doing?"

We debated between Chinese, Japanese, Thai, and American. Wings and burgers and fries won. Stu called in our order before leaving to go grab a change of clothes at his place.

"Need anything else?" he asked as he walked to the front door.

I thought a minute and shook my head.

"Okay. See you in a bit," he said walking out.

The door had barely closed when I called out. "Wait!"

He poked his head in.

"Chocolate-banana milkshake, please?"

"You got it." He smiled and closed the door.

I knew he wouldn't be gone long, so I bolted upstairs to take a quick shower. He'd only be gone about forty-five minutes, which was more than enough time if I didn't wash my hair.

When I came back downstairs, my phone rang. I assumed it was Stu and didn't look to see who it was.

"I don't *need* the milkshake," I answered.

"But you want it," Andrew responded.

"Dear Lord, what the actual *fuck* is your problem?"

"I wanted to apologize for calling you to discuss business on your personal phone."

"Ugh. Fine," I growled. "Anything else?"

"Wanna go out for dinner one night soon?"

"Eew! Why would I do that?" The thought nauseated me.

"What? You didn't enjoy our romp?"

"Whatever I may have enjoyed in the *past* doesn't apply to now." I was getting angry. "It's also inappropriate to sleep with an employee." I was lying. I had slept with Alex, but he was Joe's employee by then. That realization gave me what I was looking for to end this conversation.

"Shit. Drew, I have to call Joe back. He called earlier and I wasn't feeling well so I didn't answer. Gotta go." I ended the call before he could reply. I did have to call Joe, too, but not right that minute. Then I stared at Andrew's contact info, contemplating blocking him. But I also needed to be able to establish that we were on speaking terms when the cops pulled his phone records. It wasn't like we were good friends, but it would help for the cops to know that I may not have been the only one he'd upset with his slimy behavior.

Just as I set the phone down on the coffee table, the door opened. I leaped up and helped Stu take dinner to the kitchen. It was easier to not make a big mess and still keep things warm that way. The restaurant we ordered from had even given us paper plates.

"Score! Less dishes!" I made that gesture from the '90s that looked like I was hitting a speed bag with one fist that wasn't properly aligned—the one from the *Arsenio Hall Show*. I looked like a geek, and was totally cool with that.

Stu laughed. "You're a geek."

"I know! It's great! Did you know I read fantasy books too? Like D&D fantasy," I said.

Stu stopped taking food out of the bag in front of him and stared at me.

"What? Too much?" I giggled.

"That was the last thing I thought you'd ever say," he said. "I read fantasy too. And crime fic, because duh."

"*Dexter* and *Hannibal* are full of tips," I remarked nonchalantly.

"You don't...You *learn* from them?"

"Sure do! Mostly what not to do, but hey, sometimes they have good stuff. Plus the story lines are fucking awesome. Well, until season five of *Dexter*." I started grumbling incoherently.

"Brit, come back to reality. Let's go eat."

"K," I replied happily. As though I hadn't just gone off on some random tangent.

Stu handed me a plate containing my burger and some fries. I took it and grabbed some napkins. Then picked up my milkshake from the counter and headed for the living room.

"Come on," I said nodding.

Stu pulled a six-pack of Bud Light from another bag, taking one out of the carrier and twisting the top off. Then he picked up his plate and followed.

We sat, and Stu snatched the remote for the streaming device before I even finished tasting my milkshake. He scrolled to *Dexter* and hit play.

We ate and watched and laughed. I even yelled at the TV. I did that a lot watching horror movies, especially. But it wasn't the first time I'd done it for this show.

Stu laughed at me.

"You're the cop. Tell me that wasn't bullshit," I said.

"I guess I've gotten used to it," he replied, inhaling the remaining mouthful of burger and chewing.

I sighed and finished my burger. I was too full for wings. Apparently, Stu was too.

"I'm putting the wings in the fridge. Wanna meet here for lunch tomorrow and we can split them?" he asked as he stood up.

I hit the pause button and nodded. "Yeah. That sounds great. Are you staying here tonight?"

"Why else would I have grabbed a change of clothes?" he shot back playfully. Then he disappeared into the kitchen.

I followed and tossed my trash in the bin under the counter. Stu turned away from the fridge, kissed me, then handed me a beer.

I rubbed my stomach. "I just had a milkshake and now you're handing me a beer? Don't you know that's a bad mix?" I giggled. "Seriously, it's made me puke before."

"Well, if it makes you sick, I'll hold your hair," he offered.

"Hah. No. Maybe one beer will be okay. The last time I mixed the two, I pounded half a case before getting sick," I remarked.

Stu's face turned green. "That's gross."

"It happened. And if you want to be with me, you'll have to get use to knowing about the party girl I used to be." I kissed his cheek and walked back to the couch.

We watched a couple more episodes before Stu got up to take a shower. I turned the TV off and followed after making sure the doors were locked. Minion glared at me from a chair in the kitchen as I walked back from the door to the garage. She must have thought I was replacing her with Stu.

I reached down and petted her. "Stop that. No one could ever replace you. Especially not a human.

Come to bed." I turned the light out and went upstairs.

Stu was still in the shower when I got up there. I changed and got under the covers, though I wasn't all that tired. As the shower knobs squeaked, I flipped through to find something to watch to help my eyelids get heavy.

Stu came out wearing basketball shorts. My face made one of those expressions that he must have taken as me judging him.

"I wasn't sure how you'd feel about me getting into bed in just my underwear," he said walking over and climbing under the blanket with me.

"I'd totally mind. Because I've never seen you naked either."

"Wow! That was the most sarcasm I've heard from you in long time," he said smiling. Then he wriggled his shorts off. "Ah, that feels so much better!"

I laughed. "Can we get comfy now? After all, you're the one who said we should lie down." I tried to sound coy while making fun of him, but it came out like I was annoyed. Stu knew me well enough to know that wasn't true.

He stretched his arm out and pulled me close. I laid my head on his shoulder, and we watched dinosaurs until we fell asleep.

Fourteen

I WOKE THE NEXT morning as the sun rose. I sat up and began my morning as though nothing had changed. I got dressed for my jog but stopped at the foot of my bed before going downstairs. I watched Stu sleeping peacefully. Would he think I was even more of an asshole than he already knew me to be if I was gone when he woke up?

I walked over and kissed his cheek. His eyes opened and he smiled. "Morning, beautiful."

"Morning. I'm going for a jog. You know where the coffeemaker is. Love you," I said, kissed him again, and trotted down the stairs.

I put my sneakers on and left. Forty minutes later I came back, sweating like it was still August outside. I walked to the kitchen to drink some water before having coffee. Stu sat at the table, sipping from a mug. He smiled at me as I came in.

"I would have gone with you," he said.

"I didn't even think to ask. I'm sorry," I said before chugging a bottle of water.

"I didn't either. It's no big deal." He shrugged and sipped more coffee. "I just can't believe how lucky I am to be here with you."

"I'm the lucky one. But we won't talk about why," I said, my tone verging on bitter.

"What's wrong?" he asked.

I poured a cup of coffee and sat across from him. "I'm just mad at myself, I guess. But if I hadn't dated Sweet, we wouldn't know each other." I sipped my coffee then stared into the black depths of the coffee. "Honestly? It's still kinda weird that you came back. And I don't think there's a proper descriptor for how weird it is that you're willing to help me get away with it."

Stu smiled. "No need to be mad about any of that. What matters is that I'm here now. *And* how we move forward."

How could he be so normal about all this? What have I done to him? I pushed those questions from my mind and focused on the rest of the day.

Stu and I agreed on a time to meet back for lunch, then I went to get ready for work. Stu left after I got out of the shower. He had the afternoon shift these days, but it was still difficult to remember what the rotation was. We kissed goodbye, and I continued getting ready. Soon after, I was in my Jeep and stopping for lattes again.

Barb was at the office, as usual. When I walked in, she beamed at me.

I shielded my eyes, faking that she was blinding me. "You've gotta stop that. It's obnoxious this early." I joked as I handed her the latte.

She accepted it gratefully and sipped. "Again? Is this a new daily—" Her mouth fell open, and she gawked at me.

"Britney Cage, are you glowing?" she asked, her voice rising with each word, that timid smile daring to spread as she watched my reaction.

I shook my head and walked into my office. "I have no idea what you're talking about." I hung my purse and pulled my latte from the carrier, sipping and throwing the carrier out simultaneously. Barb followed me every step of the way. I booted up under her scrutiny.

"Spill," she ordered. That wasn't like her. Maybe Barb was a secret yenta. Or an emotional voyeur.

"I haven't told anyone yet. What makes you sure you should be the first to know?" I taunted.

"Because if you don't, I'll blind you again," she threatened. We both laughed.

"Fine." I sighed. "I wasn't here yesterday because Stu came back the night before. We talked and now…ohmigod. I have a boyfriend."

Barb screeched so loud it echoed in the reception area. "I'm so happy for you! I knew he'd come around!" She really was happy. I thought she might even cry. She did not.

"Thanks, Barb. It does feel good that he's back. Now, fill me in on what I missed."

She left and came back with a notebook. Sitting in the chair across from me, she told me about the douche client that Julie had asked the lawyer to cancel the contract negotiations with. Then she told me about how the same client came in and tried to bully her. I held a hand up, indicating I didn't want to hear any more.

"After he left, did you call the lawyer?"

She nodded.

"Was he threatening to you at all while here?"

She shook her head no. This had gotten childish.

"Why aren't you speaking? What happened?" I was mad before she opened her mouth. I picked up the receiver from its cradle, but Barb put her hand on mine.

"He yelled and stomped and carried on like a toddler throwing a temper tantrum. I told him that if he didn't leave, I'd report him for harassment and trespassing. He stomped out after that." Her face was flushed, as though thinking about it upset her.

My face softened. "Still want to report him? I don't think trespassing would stick, but we can try to press harassment charges." I shrugged. "It's up to you."

"I'll give him another chance," she said as she stood. "That was all you really missed."

"Okay. Thanks for telling me," I said, picking up the phone to call the lawyer.

Barb nodded and walked out.

"Ms. Cage, good morning. What can I do for you?" he answered.

"You can tell me what all you need from me to get this finished," I replied, a wicked grin crossing my face. I'd make sure it was known that that man came to my office and scared the shit out of my employee. It didn't matter that she didn't want to file a complaint.

He told me that it was pretty much all over now. The client had sent back whatever he needed to in order to verify that he was no longer *my* client. I was satisfied with that. And I still told him about what he'd said to Barb. He asked me to relay his sympathies to Barb about the incident.

"I'll tell her. Thanks," I said and hung up. I was still in a good mood, and that news made it better. No sooner had I replaced the receiver than the phone rang again.

"Passing Through Temp Agency, Britney Cage," I said.

"You were rude last night," Andrew said.

Knowing I'd have to tolerate his shit any longer was grating on me. I wanted to stick a stiletto where it would leave an impression. "If you say so. Again, this is unprofessional. What do you want?"

"Just that." The dial tone sounded in my ear. I rolled my head, cracking my neck. If I was merely looking forward to killing him before, now I was like a child in the back seat of a car on a long road trip. So much for going to the monastery a year ago. It had been a great experience, though. Even if I hadn't been able to apply what I'd learned.

I closed my eyes, pushing the visions of slicing An-drew's dangly bits for giggles out of my mind. I'd never thought about torture like that before. I figured he brought that out in me.

Turning to face my monitor, I got to work. Julie had sent a handful of updates in separate emails, making me smirk at how methodical and robotic she could be. I replied to all of them in a single email and she sent back a single upside-down smiley emoji.

When Barb came back from lunch, I went home for mine. Stu was there waiting for me. He got out of his black Dodge Charger wearing his uniform pants and a white T-shirt. It was hard not to ogle him. I dropped down from the driver's seat and smiled at him.

"Hey, babe! Miss me?"

"How could I not?" I responded walking to the front door.

"Ditto," he said as I unlocked the door. Once I pushed it open, Stu playfully pushed me inside and closed it behind him. We made out like high schoolers for the next thirty minutes.

I came up for air first. "It's a good thing I'm not starving."

"Would you eat me?" Stu asked.

If you only knew.

"Nah, I love you too much for that. But seriously, let's go eat. We have like thirty minutes left." I glanced at my watch and corrected myself. "Less. Come on."

I got up and walked into the kitchen. Stu followed and took the wings from the fridge. I plucked one from the container and ate it cold. It was delicious.

Stu tried one. "Not bad. Never thought I'd like cold wings, but here I am."

It was time for us to part all too soon, but I knew he'd be coming back tonight when he got off work. We kissed bye outside and walked to our vehicles.

My phone rang as I pulled out of my neighborhood.

Fifteen

I ALMOST DIDN'T ANSWER, wondering why my phone always seemed to ring at the most inopportune times. But I did.

"Brit! When will you be coming to have a meal with your old man?"

"Well, hello to you, too, Joe." I giggled. "Soon, I promise. I've just been a little out of whack lately. But hey, I've got good news. Stu came back around. He doesn't hate me. In fact, he's now my boyfriend."

"It's about damned time! Why don't the two of you come over for dinner tomorrow night? I'll even have Marsha whip up that pot roast you love so much."

I drooled as I remembered how delectable it was. "Let me check with Stu, and I'll get back to you if it'll be both of us or just me."

"You got it, kid."

"Hey, Joe?"

"What?"

"Thanks for being you," I said, pulling into the office parking lot. "I'm back at work. Call you later."

He hung up as I parked. Today had shaped up to be a pretty decent one. Even with losing a client and Andrew being Andrew. For the first time that I could remember, I was genuinely happy.

There was a bounce in my step as I walked into the reception area. I was greeted by Barb, along with two applicants waiting for interviews.

"I'll be with you shortly," I said to them, walking back to my private office. I swapped my purse for my cardigan and called the first one back. The interview was dull, as was the applicant. He'd fit the warehouse position I had open. It was a direct hire, but they wanted me to do their hiring. This kid was perfect. Athletic and said he wanted a physical job. He had the experience too. I gave him the information he needed and told him to be there Monday morning. He left, and I conducted the next interview.

This one would be going to Joe's office. It was the cashier from Publix that I'd given my number to. She was friendly and polite. It didn't hurt that she was pretty. Joe's patients would love her anyway. So would Joe.

"You start Monday," I said, handing her a sticky note with the name of the scrub store on it. "Tell them you'll be a receptionist/scheduler. They'll set you up."

She took the note and smiled at me gratefully. "Thanks, Ms. Cage. I appreciate you even considering me at all. I liked being a cashier, but the pay wasn't that great."

"I know. Customer service positions like that are tough, and the pay makes them seem worse." I smiled at her. She reminded me of Julie but younger. Not by much, but younger regardless.

She stood and reached to shake hands. I shook hers back, and she left.

The rest of the day dragged. I texted Stu after the last interview to ask if he'd be joining me at Joe's tomorrow night.

I have to work until 8. Is that too late?

No. Come after. Joe would love to get to know the man who stole his adopted daughter's heart.

Okay. See you at your place tonight when I get done. What time?

Is 8 OK?

Okay. I'll have dinner ready.

When the workday was over, Barb and I left together. I locked up as she got into her car and drove off. The sun had just started to set and was already painting the sky.

At home, I made some pasta with my signature butter sauce. Enough that there would be some for me to take to work tomorrow for lunch. If there weren't, that was okay too. It had been a while since my last hoagie anyway.

Stu walked in around a quarter after eight. "Hi, honey. I'm home!" He giggled. "I've always wanted to say that." He kissed me on the cheek.

"Good. Now that you got it out of your system, go get some pasta. I mixed the butter sauce in already, so you don't have to worry about that."

"You ate without me?" Stu feigned hurt.

"I was starving. Sorry. But I can eat more if you want," I said, planting a kiss on his forehead.

"It's fine," he said walking into the kitchen. "Want anything?"

I shook my head and flipped through the streaming channels until I found a show I needed to catch up on. It was one of the comic-book shows. Stu almost choked on his pasta when he came out.

"Superheroes too? Brit, you never cease to amaze me." He sat next to me and snagged the remote. He pressed play and continued to eat. I tried hard not to listen to the sound of his eating. Misophonia was a real thing, and I had it in a weird way.

I'd kept my squirming in check long enough for Stu to finish what was left in the pot. He'd looked at me from the corner of his eye more than once while he ate. Like he knew I was internally screaming.

"You good?" he asked coming back from the kitchen.

"I have a weird thing about being able to hear people eat is all. If I can, I get annoyed and irrationally angry. Not that me being angry is anything new."

"Fair enough. We'll have to sit farther apart or something, no biggie. Come on, let's go to bed. I'm beat." He started up the stairs as I shut the TV off.

He was in bed by the time I reached the top of the stairs. I giggled and changed before sliding in next to him. He was breathing so softly I didn't want to disturb him.

I lay there awhile, staring at the ceiling, thinking. *Is this what marriage feels like? Will he always pass out before me? Will every day be this effortless?*

Then the noise started. I made my own noise—a sort of growling snort and rolled over to face the window. Stu was snoring. I suddenly imagined smothering him. Though I hoped it was only from allergies or something. I hadn't heard it yesterday either.

Somehow, I managed to fall asleep without earplugs and woke still annoyed. With Stu's arm around me. At least there was a silver lining. I slid out of bed and changed for my jog. This time, though, I woke Stu on purpose.

"Going for a jog, want to join?"

He smiled groggily and nodded. "Yeah."

When we got outside, I noticed the nosy old bat across the street outside too.

"Fuck."

Stu followed my gaze. "Oh be nice. She's old."

"And a twat. And nosy. And I don't want to, but I try to be polite," I grumbled.

We jogged toward her, and Stu waved. She waved back and didn't try to stop us.

"You're my lucky charm," I said to him.

I heard my name being called behind us.

Sixteen

IT WAS HER; THERE was no mistaking it.

"I lied."

"What? See what she wants. Maybe it's nothing," Stu said helpfully.

I grumbled and stopped, making her come to me. Again, it was unusually hot and humid for October. The mouth inside my mind smiled maliciously.

She huffed a little when she reached us. "Good morning, Britney," she said with that air of snobbery she had.

"Morning. What can I do for you? We're jogging before work, so keep it short," I replied, refusing to hide my irritation.

"Will you be having a guest every night?"

"Will you be moving to an assisted living facility soon?" I shot back.

"Well, I never!"

"Me either."

"Not that it's really any of your business, but I'm Stu Jones, Britney's boyfriend," Stu interjected.

She looked at him, annoyance still showing on her face. "Well, Stu, thanks for letting me know. But it *is* my business since I live here too."

"Do the rules say anything about guests? If they do, point me to them so I can get the proper permission," Stu said to her. "If not, you should know Britney can always file a police report about you harassing her like this. If I'm not mistaken, you've been on her back about cops being here too, haven't you?" He arched one eyebrow.

I crossed my arms over my chest. "He's got a point. None of this is any of your business. There's nothing in the rules that says he can't be here. And I sure haven't heard you complain when there's been a patrol car here multiple days in a row. Sounds like you're just nosy. No one in here has had a single problem with prowlers or burglars except me. Maybe I will file a report." I turned slowly and started away. Stu joined me.

The neighbor huffed and walked away.

"Think I should file a report?" I asked Stu.

"If you don't, it would be a shame. At least with it on file, if she starts shit again for no reason, you can keep building a file on her." He shrugged. "Maybe even get a lawyer involved if it gets that bad. But I don't get what her issue is."

"She's just a nosy old coot with nothing else better to do than bother people who don't follow her rules. She forgets she doesn't run the association." We stopped as Stu pushed the button for the crosswalk, and waited. "Yeah, I guess I'll file a report. I'm tired of her bullshit anyway. Maybe this will get her to leave me alone."

Stu challenged me intermittently as we jogged. By the time we'd gotten back to my house, my legs felt like they would fall off, and my lungs burned as though it was my first long-distance jog. I barely spoke until I'd had two bottles of water.

"Trying to kill me?"

"I could never," Stu said smiling. "You okay?"

"Yeah. Sore and my lungs are on fire, but I'm good. I'll be taking a bath after I get home from Joe's tonight." I kissed Stu on the cheek and walked upstairs to shower and get ready for work. Stu followed.

"Are you coming tonight?" I asked him as I turned the water on.

"After work, yeah. Save me some dessert." He chuckled. "If I'm gonna jog with you, I need to keep more than one change here." He looked in the mirror at the sweat on his shirt to emphasize his point.

"Or you could join me in the shower," I said wryly as I stepped in. Stu didn't need to hear any more than that. He was being splashed with shampoo in a matter of seconds. I finished and got out while Stu stayed in a bit longer. I'd been a hog and taken over, so he'd barely had a chance to wash his face.

By the time he shut the water off, I was already dressed and downstairs feeding the cat. I came back up to put makeup on, and Stu just watched me. "You don't need that, you know."

"Well, I like it. And I've never heard you complain," I remarked with a grin. Stu nodded his acknowledgment and went downstairs. When I was finished, I did too.

We left at the same time, owing to the fact that I hadn't offered Stu a key yet. That part would come in time. It wasn't that I didn't trust him—because I did. I just needed to warm up to the idea.

The day went so fast, I'd almost forgotten to call Joe to tell him I'd definitely be there around 5:30. Instead, since it was just before four, I sent him a text. He was likely at the office or golfing, or maybe even on his way home.

He replied almost immediately. *OK. Stu coming?*
Not for dinner, but he'll be by after work.
OK. See you soon.

I was excited for Marsha's pot roast and mashed potatoes. They had been so delicious the last time I had them that as much as I wanted the recipe, I thought better of asking out of fear that I wouldn't do it justice. Hell, maybe I'd occasionally ask her to make it for me and pay her. If Joe would share her, anyway.

I left a little early to grab a bottle of wine on the way there. I knew it was unnecessary, but giving Joe flowers would have been an insult. He had a gorgeous garden, and Marsha always picked the best and brightest ones for a centerpiece.

I parked in the driveway and walked to Joe's front door. As I lifted my arm to ring the bell, the door opened. Marsha's face lit up.

"Hi, Britney! It's good to see you again! Come in," she said stepping back to let me in.

"It's good to see you too. How are you?" I smelled the roast and almost drooled all over myself as I spoke.

"I'm well, thanks," she said. Then she noticed the bottle in my hand and whispered, "Let me get that out of sight." She reached for the bottle in my hand and smirked. "You know he won't be thrilled you brought this."

I nodded. "Yep. And I don't care." I grinned.

"Don't care about what?" Joe asked walking into the foyer to greet me.

"Oh nothing," I said meeting him halfway and hugging him. Marsha took that as her cue to take the bottle to the kitchen. "You look good."

"So do you," he said pulling back. "Happy looks wonderful on you."

I frowned. "Are you gonna tell me I'm glowing too?"

"I'm sure your assistant has already told you," he said. "Come, let's catch up." He put an arm around my shoulders and led me to the dining room.

Marsha had the table set and ready for us. She'd even poured the wine I brought, and it waited in glasses at our seats. We'd always sat in the same places, Joe and I. Him at the end by the entry to the kitchen and me off the corner to his left. He pulled the chair out for me to sit, which made me think something was off.

I waited for him to sit, then asked. "Joe, what's going on?'

His face screwed up in confusion. "What do you mean?"

"The last time you pulled a chair out for me, you had bad news," I chided.

Joe sighed. "I really don't have any bad news this time. Actually, it's all good things to tell you."

I raised an eyebrow. "In that case, share away." I smiled.

"First, let's toast to your continued happiness. And that you've finally managed to pull your head out of your ass enough to see that Stu is good for you and so is your growing relationship with him." I snickered and raised my glass, tapping his.

We sipped and Joe continued. "That new girl you sent over is fabulous. The clients seem to like her a lot. I think I'll be looking into keeping her if she continues this way."

"I figured she'd be a shoo-in. She's really just happy and perky. I'm almost jealous." I chuckled.

Marsha came out to see if either of us needed more wine or anything else. "Dinner's almost finished too."

We thanked her, and she left the room. "Joe, I'm inviting her to eat with us," I said when the door closed.

"Not tonight. I already asked. She claims to have had a big lunch." He sounded like he didn't believe her.

"Maybe she's just not hungry," I said. "I'll talk to her later. I'd love to get to know her more."

"That's sweet of you, Brit."

"Back to you catching me up," I said and took a swig of wine.

Marsha brought dinner out as Joe talked about his latest appointment with his cardiologist. That had been the best checkup Joe had had since his heart attack. He credited more golfing.

I credited Marsha. She took care of him like he was her family, not her employer. I really appreciated that he listened to her more than he did to me. As long as she was getting through to him was all that mattered.

We enjoyed our dinner, and Joe talked some more. His kids had called him and sent photos of his grandchildren. He paused eating and excitedly showed them off. They were cute kids.

"So what else is new with you? Better yet, what made you decide that a relationship was okay all of a sudden?"

I almost choked. Then I cleared my throat. "Like you said, I pulled my head out of my ass." We both got a good chuckle from that.

"Touché," he replied.

"Really, though, I just decided to take a chance. He made me realize that the time we were already spending together was perfect and that things would move forward on their own. I drank a lot in the time he wasn't talking to me. But now I only drink socially or a glass here or there. I feel good."

Joe nodded. "Well, I'm glad you stopped drinking so much. I'd hate to have to come visit you in the hospital."

I smiled. Marsha brought dessert out and set it on the table while I was updating Joe on client issues and the neighbor lady who was in my business.

When I realized that Marsha had set a fresh pie down, I glanced at my watch. It was as though the man had ESP or something because the doorbell rang. I jumped up, intending to answer it. Joe waved me to sit back down.

"Sit, relax."

I poured wine for the three of us. Stu walked into the dining room as I set the empty bottle back on the table. He kissed me on the cheek and shook Joe's hand. Then he sat across the corner to Joe's right.

"Thanks for having us," Stu said to Joe, eyeing the pie.

"Of course! How are you, Stu?"

I wanted pie, and I knew Stu did too, so I took the plates and placed slices on each, then handed them back. The men chatted happily. I kept myself out of it for as long as possible. Then Joe made a dad joke and I rolled my eyes.

"That's a good one, Joe," Stu said laughing.

"Don't encourage him," Marsha said, coming in from the kitchen. "Can I get you anything else?"

We all shook our heads, mouths full of pie. Marsha smiled knowingly and walked back into the kitchen.

When I finished, I stood and took my dishes into the kitchen. It was the only way I could thank Marsha for being slick about the wine without Joe hearing. I opened the door, but Joe spoke to me halfway through it, making me pause.

"She wasn't as slick as you think she was. I know you brought the wine," he said.

I turned my head enough to catch the grin on his face. I shrugged and continued on my path.

"Did you hear what he just said?" I asked Marsha.

She was loading the dishwasher. "I did. That man…" She giggled as she straightened up. "He doesn't miss a thing, does he?"

I shook my head, handing her my plate. "Nope. Never really has." *Except one thing.*

"Maybe next time you can join us," I said to her.

"I'd like that." She smiled back at me.

Whether she meant it or not, I had a feeling she'd find excuses to not join us. I glanced at the clock on the oven. "It was good to see you. I'm gonna get out of here. Thanks for trying to hide the wine for me."

"Any time," she replied and hugged me.

Back in the dining room, I hugged Joe. "It's late. We should go so you can get to bed."

"Getting proper sleep has become more important than I ever imagined," Joe replied standing. "I'll walk you out."

Stu stood and held my hand as we walked to the front door. I hugged Joe again when we got there. "Thank you."

"Any time, dear," he replied.

Stu shook his hand and thanked him also. Then we left, me getting into my Jeep, him getting into his Charger. We didn't have to speak about it; it was understood that Stu was coming back to my house.

When we got there, we changed and lay in bed watching a movie for a while. A doorbell rang and we paid it no mind. It fit the scene. The second time, it did not.

Seventeen

Stu looked at me. I had no definite answer, but I had a suspicion.

"I'll get it." I huffed and snorted as I threw the blanket off of myself. My face wore that expression that said I'd stab someone just for being at my front door for some stupid reason.

"Expecting someone?" Stu asked.

"No. I just know who thinks they can just show up whenever they fucking want," I replied angrily.

Andrew's face was red, and he was swaying when I opened the door.

"Hey, baybuh! What's going on?" he cheerfully greeted me.

"Go the fuck away," I said, emphasizing every word.

"Aww, that's no way to greet an old friend." He flashed a cheesy grin. "Aren't you gonna let me in?"

"Absolutely not. Why are you here?" I didn't even know why I hadn't slammed the door in his face yet.

"You know why," he said. He tried to be coy, but he sounded like he was an actor in a B-movie.

"Go the fuck away," I repeated. Then I heard footsteps down the stairs. *Now you're in trouble, fuck head.*

Stu pulled the door farther open, and I glared at him. "Sorry," he said, realizing I was thinking that Minion might try to run. I looked around for her but didn't see her. Stu saw me checking and said, "She's under the blanket on the bed." I relaxed.

"You," he said to Andrew, "I believe she told you to leave. Twice." He was firm; not mean but firm.

Andrew looked from me to Stu and back. "Who're you?" he slurred.

"It doesn't matter. Go. Now. Before I call the cops." I was getting angry at that point.

Andrew held his hands up in the defensive position. "Okay, okay, I'm going." He turned around and started to walk down the walkway. Then he turned back. "You sure you don't want to *play*?"

I growled and slammed the door, scraping Stu's nose. "Sorry," I said to him.

"Who was that?" he asked as we walked back upstairs. He rubbed his nose a little.

I made that snorting growl noise of annoyance I had a habit of making at times like these. "*That* was Andrew York. We had a few flings a while back. We literally ran into each other one day while I was jogging. It was after I told you about my...other self. He's been trying to get back into my pants since then. He's next to die."

Stu snickered. "Well, I can see why. The guy can't seem to take no for an answer."

We got back into bed, and Stu looked at me with that goofy grin of his. "That came out so easily."

At first, I wasn't sure what he was referring to. Then it hit me. "It did, didn't it?" I sat up and looked at the tip of his nose then kissed the tiny speck of a red spot the door had left. "I guess I'm more than comfortable with you knowing my plans." I rested my head on his shoulder.

He ran his fingers through my hair. "So, what are your plans, anyway?"

"Well, I know how he's going to die, and I know how I want to dispose of the body...All that's really left is where." I thought about that. As far as I knew, the garage in Ybor was still vacant. I could have Andrew meet me there, or I could even drive us. I knew it would come to me without much stressing or thinking about it. "I don't really want to talk about it. Like, yeah, you can know, but to talk about it is just weird for me. If that makes sense?"

"It does. Talking about it is weird for me too. I want to know your plans, and curiosity is making me want to be there when you do whatever it is you do, but I doubt I can watch. That may make it a lot harder for me to be any kind of cool about it."

I knew what he was saying without him having to elaborate. I knew he wanted to know details. I also knew he *didn't* want to know details. I felt the same way about talking about it.

I closed my eyes and just enjoyed Stu continuing to run his fingers in my hair.

The next time I opened my eyes, I had a crick in my neck, and it was daylight.

I grumbled and rolled over, trying not to move my stiff neck too much. "Shit," I mumbled, bringing my hand up to attempt a massage after I'd gotten half-comfortable.

Stu must have heard or felt me or something because his hand took over for mine. "Shh. I know it hurts. Always does. But you slept like a rock. I wasn't about to wake you."

"Thanks, I think. I probably would've been mad if you woke me up, so…" The massage felt good and was loosening the tightness that had caused the initial pain. "That feels so good."

Stu rubbed his fingers in circular motions for a few more minutes. When he stopped, my eyes popped open. "Aww, why'd you stop?" I whined exaggeratedly.

Stu chuckled. "Because it's well past time to get a good jog in before you go to work." He rolled over and kissed my cheek.

"Bah! I don't have to jog today," I replied.

"It's almost eight," he said.

"Oh. In that case, I guess it's time to get out of bed." I slid out from under the blanket slowly until Stu pulled it off of me altogether. "You're the worst!" I joked.

"I'm a contradiction," he quipped.

I shook my head and went to get the coffee started. When I came back up, Stu was brushing his teeth. As I picked out an outfit, I heard him start the shower. As much as I loved all of this novelty, I knew there would come a time that it would annoy the ever-loving fuck out of me. For now, though, I decided to enjoy every bit I could. Reason also told me to remain somewhat cautious. Good things generally didn't last, and that much was already proven by Joe's heart attack earlier this year.

I got in the shower when Stu got out and was ready for work before I knew it. We kissed and parted ways again. On my way into the office, I pondered him moving in with me.

The day moved at warp speed. By lunch, Julie had emailed me to let me know that the client whose information I'd sent had decided to sign on. She told me he'd be more than happy with the standard contract for one temp. He would add more if he needed to. I was more than pleased by the outcome. I'd already suspected he'd join us but wanted to be sure. Julie's lunch with him had solidified that.

After I hit the send button on my email reply to Julie, I sent a text in the existing group conversation calling for a girls' night.

Y'all. It's been too damnned long. When are we going to The Pub?

I'd gotten so lost in emails and phone calls, I didn't have time to look at my phone until it was quitting time. The girls had had a discussion about days and ultimately agreed on tomorrow night at seven.

Awesome! Can't wait! I sent back.

By the time I'd finished my work, Barb had already said bye to me and left. I'd been so deep in everything, I don't think it even registered that she was gone. I laughed at myself and headed home.

Eighteen

I'D HALF EXPECTED STU to be waiting for me when I got home. He was not. I sighed, relieved. Then I scolded myself for feeling that way. Maybe I wasn't ready for our relationship to have escalated this much.

I fed Minion and made some pasta for myself. Stu texted saying he had something to do and he was sorry he couldn't be here.

Don't worry about it, I responded.

I wondered if I'd ever get used to him being around all the time. Did I even want that? Then I remembered how sad I was when he wasn't around at all. I couldn't handle that again, so I decided to take things as they came and see what happened.

There wasn't much, but the house needed to be straightened up, and basic cleaning was necessary. To work off the crazy amount of carbs I'd eaten, that's precisely what I did. And when I was finished, I showered and went to bed. Alone.

It was a weird feeling, and I had more trouble than I expected falling asleep. I turned the TV on and watched a few movies. I even got out of bed to retrieve the book I'd left on the coffee table to read it in bed—with a movie on in the background. By the time I'd managed to be tired enough to lie down, it was 3 a.m. I placed the book on the night table and closed my eyes.

My phone rang and against my better judgment, I opened my eyes enough to answer it.

"Hello?" I sounded like a frog.

"Brit," Julie said, "did I wake you?"

"Yeah. What time is it?"

"Seven. Look, I'm swinging by your office to drop the signed contract off to you. I should be there around 9:30. Do you have anything scheduled?"

I fought the sleep fog that shrouded my brain to recall if I did. "Not that I can think of. See you then," I replied.

"Okay, bye." Julie hung up.

I was equal parts mad and glad that she'd called and woken me up. Had she not, I wondered if I'd have woken up on time. I rolled out of bed and went downstairs. This morning was the same as any other, and I went back upstairs with a cup of coffee. It wouldn't be enough, but when had it ever been really?

At least I was awake enough to drive. Traffic was the worst it had been in a while, but I'd also left a few minutes later than I usually did. Only those who fought rush hours understood that struggle.

I shuffled through the door and it chimed, but Barb was nowhere to be seen.

"Be right there!" she called from the kitchen.

"It's just me," I replied. "But if you're making coffee, can I please have a cup?"

"Sure thing!"

I slipped into my office and down into my chair. My head lolled a bit, and my eyes threatened to close. Barb walked in just in time. She set the cup down in front of me.

"Drink," she said. "Now. Before you fall asleep."

"Thanks," I muttered. I took a sip, and my brain popped once, like a carbureted engine trying to start in the winter. Another sip, and the engine kicked over. "Barb, you're a lifesaver!"

She smiled and went back out to her desk.

I got to work after chugging what was left in the cup, right about the same time the door chimed. I heard Barb and Julie greet each other and exchange pleasantries.

I called out, "Hey, Jules!" to let them know I was cool with her coming back without being announced. But it was Julie. When would I have ever cared about that?

Julie came in, and I stood to hug her. She had brought coffee and handed it to me first.

"God, I love you," I said.

I hugged her. When she let go, she set the envelope containing the signed contract on my desk. I downed half of the coffee.

"I'm so excited for tonight! It's been a while since we've all gotten together," she commented.

"Yeah, really. I may get there early just because. Might even throw back some coffee to help me stay awake," I said with a giggle. "Time to sit?"

"No, I have to get to the office. I just wanted to say hi, I love you, and drop this off."

We hugged again and she left.

By lunchtime, I was falling asleep again. Not only had I asked Barb to pick some up for me, but I ran across the street to get another. It was one of those 20-oz. cups too. If need be, I could make more at the office. I snagged a few energy drinks for good measure. I'd forgotten how my nearly thirty-year-old brain reacted to having little sleep.

Finally, it was time to close up shop. I couldn't recall another time I'd been this excited to do so, either. Barb and I left together, as we had been for days now. She waved bye as she drove away, and I locked the door.

I jumped in my Jeep and hightailed it home. Traffic seemed light, which made me happier than I already was.

I parked in my driveway, ran inside, and made more coffee before feeding the cat and changing. By 6 p .m., I'd downed another half pot. I hadn't bothered keeping track of exactly how much caffeine I'd consumed, but I knew it was barely enough. Then something in my brain snapped—I guessed it was the excitement kicking in—and I woke up more than I'd have hoped. I was ready for the night and to see my girls again.

On my way out the door, I grabbed my purse and phone. However, I hesitated to open the door. Given Andrew's penchant for just showing up lately, I opted to run upstairs to take my Glock out. I placed the holster inside my pants and slid the gun in. It felt strange, but it was also the first time in months I could remember feeling an actual *need* to carry. I hadn't yet conducted my purse carry research either.

I felt better about opening the door and potentially being accosted. I heaved a great sigh when I saw no one outside. I locked up and took off for the mall.

I pulled into the valet drop-off and got out. The valet handed me a ticket as I walked away.

The walk to The Pub wasn't long, and I found myself picking up the pace the closer I got. When I opened the door and walked in, I was assaulted by the smells of the fresh food and the sounds of happy people.

The hostess noticed me and shrieked. "Britney! Hey! It's been a while! How are you?"

"I'm great! How are you? Oh! It'll be the five of us, as usual," I said.

"Okay. Your room is being cleaned now. There was a group in there, but they just left. I'm great, thanks. School is kicking my ass this semester," she lamented.

"I had a few classes like that. What are you going for? I don't remember if you ever told me."

"Nursing," she said. "It's a stable job and pays better than most others. Plus I like helping people."

"Nice. Any specific practice, or does it not matter?"

"Doesn't matter," she said shaking her head and smiling.

The busser came down the stairs and nodded to me. "It's clean!" he called over the noise.

I nodded back at him and handed the hostess a twenty, "Thanks, doll."

Her expression said shock, but I'd always tipped her pretty well. I appreciated that she'd always taken care of us and made sure we had the same table as much as possible. She handed me some menus, and I walked upstairs.

I'd just gotten comfortable when a server walked up. He was new and friendly. He took my drink order—coffee, water, and a mojito—looked at me funny, and walked away.

Julie arrived next, followed by Sarah, then Danielle and Kristen. The server was in shock that he'd been gone only a few minutes and had come back to a table full of women. I caught him stealing glances at Kristen. After he'd left with all of their drink orders, I mentioned it.

"Kristen, I think you have an admirer," I said giggling.

"I wonder if he'll expect breakfast in the morning," she said dryly. The table erupted into laughter. It was an ongoing joke that we all had. Years ago, Kristen had met some guy in a bar, and she took him back to her place. He actually expected her to cook him breakfast in the morning *and* needed a ride home. That guy had been a piece of work. Their "relationship" didn't last long, either.

We chatted some more, and when the server came back we all ordered food.

The server joked. "You sure you ladies are gonna eat all that?"

"Damn right," Kristen answered. "If not, maybe you can share it with me later." She was slick; I had to give her that. The kid's face flushed, and he practically ran away. We all got another good giggle.

"So, I wanted to tell you all some really good news," I said. All of their eyes bored into me. "Stu and I are together."

The girls cheered and toasted. "Told you so," Kristen said.

"Yeah, yeah." I lifted my mojito in celebration that we were all together on such short notice. "Ladies, let's toast to good friends together again."

They each raised a glass and cheered.

The night went by entirely too fast. Especially for it being the first in over a month. Under normal circumstances, if we'd had to wait this long for a night out, we'd have shut the place down. Tonight, however, we finished our food and drinks, and left around 10:30 p.m.

I found myself grateful for the early night. I'd barely slept last night and needed to catch up.

We hugged our good-nights at the valet stand, with me waiting for my Jeep. The rest of the girls had parked themselves, so they just walked out to their cars. The valet pulled my Jeep up and hopped out. As we walked past each other, I handed him a ten. It was the only way I could really express gratitude for taking care of my ride.

When I got home, I fed Minion, then all but ran upstairs to change and lie down. Before I could attempt to sleep, though, I texted the group to let them know I was home. They responded that they were too. We said we'd do it again soon, and the conversation stopped for the night.

I lay down and closed my eyes, imagining the things to come.

Nineteen

IT WAS LIKE STU had come back at the perfect time. Stalking Andrew would start this week. And I expected it wouldn't last too long.

First, I had to find out how much Jim wanted him around. Since I'd heard nothing, I called for an update.

"Britney! Hey! I was just thinking about you. How are you? Barb says the two of you have had some serious caffeination days," he said with a chuckle.

"We have. It's been interesting," I admitted. "So, how's life with Andrew? I haven't heard anything from either of you, so I wanted to check in."

"As bummed as I'd be if I lost him, I'd probably be okay with it too," he said.

"Okay. I've got others I can send," I said, scrolling through my database for suitable matches. "I'm pretty sure I've got a few looking for something potentially permanent."

"No rush, Britney. Like I said before, he does really good work."

"Well…hmm…How about I send you a few to talk to and go from there? I'll even handle the scheduling. Well, Barb will." I giggled. "Just let me know what works for you."

"Thanks, Britney. You don't have to do all that—"

"I do," I said. "It's literally my job."

Jim chuckled. "I guess it is. Okay. I'll send you an email in a bit. I have to check my schedule."

"Of course! We'll send you the appointment list once it's complete. Thanks, Jim. Have a good day."

"Thank you, Ms. Cage. You too."

I hung up and called Barb's extension to let her know what was going on.

"Oh! I didn't know it wasn't working out," she commented.

"I guess Jim wanted to keep him. He did say that he really likes the work Andrew does. But I get how difficult Andrew can be. I've known him a long time. Even I have problems with him from time to time."

"Oh wow…Okay, I'll get on this list and send it back. Do you want me to update the temps' info if they're unavailable?"

"Please?"

"You got it." Barb hung up.

I smiled and fought the urge to rub my hands together like a cartoon villain. The plan was coming along nicely. I'd start the stalking either tonight or tomorrow night. Stu would understand why I wouldn't be available. Plus, it would give him time to plan things out on his end. Though I did have one thing still out of place: the boat. Maybe Stu would have an idea about that. Or we could come up with something together.

Again, when I got home at the end of the day, Stu was not at my house waiting for me. I hadn't even talked to him at all yet. So I called him. He didn't answer, and I didn't leave a message. I did text him "I love you" and left it at that. I continued through my evening routine and changed before heading out to Andrew's neighborhood.

I knew that the office he was working in closed around six. That gave me time to get there and find a good spot to sit where he wouldn't see me. There was also a park close enough for me to leave my Jeep and walk to Andrew's. That was the easier choice for this night. I didn't plan to be there long anyway. But just long enough to see around what time he got home. The following week or so would tell me everything else I needed to know.

I drove around his block first, looking for a parking spot that I might be able to watch from without him seeing me. Then I realized how stupid that was. He knew my Jeep and knew his neighborhood. So I drove a few streets down and looked for a place to park that wasn't visible from the main drag.

I'd found a cul-de-sac that fit what I was looking for but no empty parking space. So I drove over to the park and left my Jeep there. Hoofing it to Andrew's was the only real option for now. It would also make it a little easier to remain out of sight.

Back on Andrew's block, there was a palm tree that had fallen halfway over. The property it was on held no buildings, just a retention pond. I didn't have any bug spray and made a mental note to put some on next time. Even if the plan were to find a place to sit and remain inside my Jeep. Somehow, I felt that would be next to impossible, though.

The sun started to set as I sat in the grass behind the palm. Mosquitoes and chiggers and other biting bastards were beginning to make their presence known. I peeked out and noticed I somehow missed Andrew pulling into his driveway. I must've been slapping bugs away. He couldn't have come in a different way because there was only one road in and out.

I didn't want to risk being caught due to extensive bug bites, so I walked back to my Jeep. I scratched the whole seven-minute drive home too. When I got inside, I tore through what I had for a bath, but none of it would help the itching. So I ran to the drugstore on the corner and found oatmeal bath. It was pricey, but all that mattered at that point was soothing the itch. The last thing I needed was for someone to ask why I was covered in insect bites and welts on top of stalking *my* prey.

The bath felt good; the itching seemed to reduce but not disappear altogether. I'd survive. But I'd need to sit in my Jeep to watch him if I didn't want to draw eyes by scratching myself constantly. Maybe daytime stalking would be better. Or…

I grabbed my phone and called Stu. He answered on the first ring.

"Hey, babe. What's up?"

"Can I borrow your car?"

"Straight to the point. Sure. Can I ask why?"

"Yeah. I have to watch Andrew so I can knock him out and kidnap him. It's part of my KKD—kidnap, kill, dispose—process. Anyway, he knows my Jeep and I got bit to hell tonight sitting outside."

Stu giggled. "Oatmeal bath helps. So does bug spray. But yes, you can absolutely borrow my car. Just this once. How long do you need it for?"

"Like a week, tops."

"Promise not to let him in my car?"

"Duh. I'll drug him inside my Jeep. I'm not planning to take him from his house, anyway."

"Less to have to hide, I suppose. Don't tell me any more. I don't want to know. I'll come swap vehicles tomorrow at your office. Sound good?"

"Sounds great! Thank you, babe."

"Just this once. Don't make me regret it, either. I love you."

"Love you too," I said and hung up.

The bonus was that Stu's car had tinted windows. As beneficial as that was, I also had slight difficulty seeing out of them when driving. I just wasn't used to the darkness. On the way to and from Andrew's, I'd have to keep the windows down enough to be able to drive. I hoped I'd get used to it within a day or two because it was still hot as hell outside. October heat waves were no joke.

I crawled under the blanket and tried to sleep, but I couldn't. At least not right away. I was still too itchy. So I ran to the drugstore again and picked up some bite-relief something. I found a pen thing that claimed to help, so I grabbed two. Then I went back home and played color the dots—it was a twisted version of connect the dots, but it worked. The itching calmed considerably once the stuff dried.

I crawled back under the blanket and fell asleep.

For the first time in a long time, I was woken up by a nightmare. It was basically a replay of when Sweet broke in and I shot him. But in the nightmare, it was Andrew, and I was home and asleep. And both of my guns and my kill knife were in the safe. I was basically defenseless, save a pen on the nightstand. So I'd stabbed him in the eye with it, buying myself time to unlock my safe and shoot him.

I slid from bed and rinsed my face, then went back to sleep. Or I tried to. It took another hour or so of staring at the ceiling. But I finally fell back to sleep.

Three hours later, I woke up to my alarm. So much for real sleep. I'd have to call it a night early again if I wanted to stop drinking so much caffeine in the hopes of keeping myself awake. I'd done that in college, and it didn't work out so well. I'd fallen asleep in class and gotten kicked out of it for a week. I didn't want to leave Barb alone to run the office while I kicked myself out for a week. I didn't think she'd be able to handle it.

I got ready for work, deciding to dress down, instead of in my usual business attire. Jeans and a nice blouse did the trick, and I still looked professional. Not like in the magazines, but I looked good.

I'd been at the office about three hours when Stu arrived. Barb was so shocked to see him that she didn't quite announce his entry. Instead, she made weird noises that sounded like, "Sue...here...you...Cage." It made Stu and I both giggle as he walked into my office.

He dropped his keys on the desk in front of me.

I nodded to the coat rack I kept my purse on. "You can fish them out or bring the purse over. It's up to you."

He smirked and pulled the purse down, walking over and setting in in front of me. "You know how us men are. We won't go in a woman's purse, even if she tells us to."

I sneered at him and took my keys out. Then I fiddled with them to get my house key off. "Can't have this...yet," I said jiggling it in front of my face.

Stu sighed. "I don't want my own right now. We need to adjust to just being together. That's why I haven't been calling or texting a lot lately. I don't want to be clingy or anything."

I nodded. "Thank you. I feel the same. I'm glad you came back, but I definitely need time to adjust."

He kissed me on the cheek then turned to leave. "Call you later. I've got errands to run. Love you." Then the door chimed, signaling his exit.

"Love you too," I said to thin air.

Twenty

THREE DAYS OF NIGHT stalking and two of following him through his day found me the perfect time to get Andrew to willingly get into my Jeep. A dinner meeting was the lie I'd planned to tell him. And it wouldn't be a full lie. I'd take him somewhere alright. To the garage in Ybor.

The day I'd planned to KKD Andrew, I met Stu for lunch at my house. Presumably, we'd switch back to our vehicles. While there, I'd tell him my plan for disposal. I needed an idea from him. What I got was unexpected.

"Well, I can pay cash for the boat rental. I'll even use my real name. We're going fishing. No bigs. I also know about a dock that doesn't have cameras. Over on that side—particularly that city—they don't have much crime, so they have no need for cameras *every-where*. Sure, places have them. But there are docks that don't, so we'll be alright." He cleared his throat. "A romantic nighttime boat ride for m'lady." He held his hand out to me and bowed.

I laughed. "You're incorrigible! I love it! Thank you." I wrapped my arms around the back of his neck and kissed him hard. So hard I bit his lip. "Sorry!"

He blotted the broken skin with the back of his hand. "If you're still hungry, we can grab something to eat." He joked. *If you only knew.*

"Okay, so are we meeting somewhere or…" I trailed off.

"I'll call you with the address. We can meet there tonight if you want," he replied. "I'll head over that way in about an hour."

"Okay." We kissed again before parting ways.

After work, I met Andrew in the parking lot where he parked for work. He was surprised to see me.

"Get in," I said. "We're overdue for a professional meeting."

"If that doesn't sound ominous," he replied.

"It's not. Promise," I said crossing my heart with two fingers.

He eyed me suspiciously. "Trying to seduce me?"

I snorted. "Yeah. You caught me. Pig. Get in the damned truck." I nodded toward the passenger seat.

Andrew ran around the front to get in, needing no more prodding. I could have easily run him over, but that would likely have been too obvious. He closed the door and clicked his seatbelt. Then he turned his head in my direction.

"I quit," he said flatly.

"You what?" I asked, driving off.

"I quit. Gave Jim my notice today."

"Why?"

He shrugged. "I appreciate your help and all, and I like Jim when he's not being a dick, but the job got monotonous."

"Andrew, accounting jobs are usually monotonous," I replied.

"I know. That's part of why I quit. I don't want to do it anymore." He looked out the window, not seeming to care that we were on I-275 headed toward Ybor.

"Oh," I said, trying to keep up a civil conversation. "So what will you do? Do you want another temp spot somewhere?"

"Nah. Working for you has its issues, most of which I'm responsible for."

"At least you can admit it," I commented.

"But I'm not apologizing for it. I still think you want me."

Gross.

"I have a boyfriend, Andrew. But the friend zone never did have an effect on you."

I got off at my exit, Andrew finally taking notice of where we were. I stopped at the red light at the intersection of the ramp.

"Whe—"

I jabbed him in the neck with a syringe of ketamine. In seconds, his head lolled, and he was out cold.

I drove to the garage and—just like I'd done with Alex—I got out to open the bay door and brought my Jeep in. Then I pulled the bay door closed and locked it. Andrew was still out, making it easy for me to pull the beat-up desk and cover it with plastic.

By the time I'd gotten my bag ready near the table, Andrew stirred.

"Hey, big guy! Come on down here," I said pulling him down to step on the ground. He wobbled, and I put his arm around my shoulders to guide him. "I've got a surprise for you. How do you feel about being taped to a table?"

He was still groggy, and my question barely registered. He slurred a response I couldn't understand.

"I'll take that as a yes." I helped him sit on the table and laid him back gently. Not that it would have mattered much if he bumped his head. I wanted to beat the shit out of him, but that would make him wake up quicker from the hormone rush. *That* was the opposite of what I needed.

Once he was on his back, I taped him down with duct tape, leaving his mouth free to spout out things he thought were insulting; things I'd most likely laugh at. Things like calling me a fucking whore, saying I liked it every time we were together, and my personal favorite, begging for his life that I wouldn't spare. If anyone heard him, they wouldn't think anything of it. I placed the tape on the vehicle lift and messed around in my bag for my knife. I also took out two contractor bags.

"Brit…what…What's going on?" He was starting to come around. "Why can't I move?"

I laughed. Not just at him but at the situation he'd found himself in.

"You have an issue with the word *no*, Andrew. Mainly when it comes from women. When they tell you to fuck off or that they won't sleep with you. I see you have that problem when it comes to me. So I wonder"—I paused and ran the tip of the knife under his eye—"are you that pushy with all women, or is it just me? Keep in mind, your answer won't stop me from killing you. Call me curious."

"You fucking BITCH!" he yelled. His eyes were filled with a mixture of anger and fear. "How dare you think that YOU could keep turning ME down!" He fought the duct tape. I laughed harder. "I'm gonna fucking kill you, you fucking cunt!"

"Aww, you're sweet," I mocked. I watched him wriggle and fight some more then raised the knife in both hands. "I won't miss you, Andrew. To be honest, I don't think anyone will."

I slammed the knife down into his chest. Blood started to pool in the center divot of his chest, under the pommel. There was just enough life left in him that he looked at me with genuine sadness in his eyes. Then the light in them flickered out. It always amazed me how easily that light in someone's eyes went out. As though their life was nothing more than a candle. I supposed that was true of all life, human or not.

I pulled the knife out and pulled the plastic up around Andrew's lifeless body. Then I washed my knife in the parts cleaner with soap and water before putting it away. I took the duct tape roll off the lift and wrapped it around the plastic, trying not to get too much blood on the ground. Then I pulled one contractor bag over his head, stopping when it made me.

The other I pulled over his feet. The bags overlapped a few inches in the middle. I taped them together, too, in an effort not to get blood all over the inside of my Jeep.

I left him on the desk while I opened the back door. There was a tarp I kept back there for times like these, so I unfolded and covered everything up as much as the tarp allowed. Then I went back to Andrew's body and squatted down to lift him over my shoulders like a scarf. He was heavier than he looked, and I stumbled more than once.

But I got to my Jeep, then dropped him inside. He landed with a *thump*. I maneuvered him into a sort of sitting fetal position and closed the door. The spare tire did a fantastic job blocking him from view. I smiled and finished cleaning up.

I checked my phone when I was finished. No missed calls or texts from Stu. I shrugged and got into the driver's seat. I wasn't sure what else to do other than wait. He'd said he'd call or text the address for me to head to. I could've started on I-4, but I only knew to take it all the way to I-95. Or I could've taken the back roads that were mostly unlit and potentially littered with wildlife. I decided to wait until I heard from Stu and turned the radio on.

I rocked out but kept the volume down. I wasn't trying to draw any more attention than Andrew's screaming may have. Around twenty minutes later, I got a text from Stu with an address. I plugged it into the GPS on Andrew's phone and backed out of the garage, closed and locked the bay door, and got on the road.

Twenty-One

Once I'd gotten onto I-4, I thought better of it and rerouted to the back roads. Whether they were lit at night or not, I wasn't fucking around and getting stuck in bumper-to-bumper traffic for three hours in Orlando. This was a more scenic route, too.

I'd gassed up before luring Andrew, so I'd be good for the whole trip there. Maybe on the way back, in the daylight, I'd fill up, but I'd been getting decent fuel mileage lately, so I wasn't overly concerned.

The ride alone was a lonely one. Probably because I was excited to see Stu. I was also nervous. Having him there for the body dump was a weird thing to think about. Add that to the paranoia that had been coming and going, and I was untrusting of Stu again.

"FUCK!" I screamed and beat on the steering wheel. "What is *wrong* with me?!"

Instead of thinking about it, I chose to talk to myself. The conversation was ludicrous, with me going back and forth with myself. Arguing if I should be freaking out or not. It was awful. I turned the music up then down again and called Stu.

"Hey, babe, what's up? On your way?"

"What the fuck, man? Why are you doing this to me?" I whined.

"Whoa. Britney, calm down. Why am I doing what? Are you okay?"

"No! I'm not! I don't trust you," I said, nearly bursting into tears.

"What can I do to help you see that I'm not going to arrest you or turn you in? I really do love you and want to be with you. Maybe my morals are gray instead of black and white." He sighed. "I always thought they were, that decisions were either right or wrong. Then I fell in love with you, and you told me who—or what—you are. It's all gray now."

I growled and wanted to throw something, but I was driving. I trusted Stu but only to a point, it seemed. It was too late to back out now. I had to either take my chances or blow him off. "Arg! I'll be there soon…"

"You don't sound very sure of that," Stu said.

"I'm not. But I don't know what else to do. I hadn't exactly planned to have another trust issue pop up." I growled again.

"Brit, I swear—"

I hung up. Neither one of us had nothing to say that could make me feel better. If, on the way to Stuart, I noticed a low-flying plane or that I was being followed, I'd know for sure that Stu was lying to me.

Three hours later, and I was pulling into the parking lot of the dimly lit marina. I backed in next to Stu's car and unlocked the doors. Stu climbed in.

"I was worried about you," he said looking into my eyes. "How do you feel?"

I shrugged. "I feel like I wasn't followed. Beyond that, I'm not entirely sure. But I'm here."

"Good." He leaned over and kissed me. I kissed him back. Again, I felt like I could trust him. *What is going on with you?* My brain and my heart were connected, but that link was sputtering in and out. I wasn't in a great place. But I still had Andrew in the back and needed to feed the fish.

I looked around and then at Stu. "Where's the boat?"

Stu turned his head and pointed to a boat that, from this distance, looked similar to Dexter's. I couldn't see the name and honestly didn't care. I cared about getting this asshole out of my Jeep and into a place no one would find him for a very long time, if at all.

I turned the engine off, and Stu got out as I did. I jumped down and pulled my bag from the back. I hoped I wouldn't have to use my knife again, and I wasn't prepared to. But I would if it came down to it. I slung it over my shoulder as Stu opened the back door.

"Nice wrap job," Stu complimented me.

"Thanks," I said nonchalantly. "It's kinda part of what I do."

Stu's face lit up. Not out of excitement or love or anything obvious. I suspected it was the rush of his first body dump.

"Doesn't feel like you thought it would, huh?" I asked.

He hoisted Andrew's still-bagged, limp form over one shoulder. "No. It's exhilarating. I honestly thought I'd get sick and throw up, "he said. "I…this feels…good."

I smiled as I closed and locked the Jeep. *Maybe he's not gonna arrest you after all.*

"This way," Stu said, walking to the rental.

It was a twenty-seven-foot Bayliner named *Patrick's Square*. I giggled.

"What's so funny?" Stu asked.

"The name of the rental. Either I'm reading it wrong, or the person who named it may have a thing for fictional serial killers."

Stu stared at me blankly. I laughed and climbed aboard. I looked around and opened the doors to go below deck. I stopped short and turned to Stu. "Did you already open her up? The doors were unlocked."

"Yeah," he answered, dropping Andrew's body onto the seat to catch his breath. "I had to check it when the guy handed the keys over. So I left it open to make it easier for us." He picked Andrew up again and walked downstairs. He set the body on the first seat available.

The boat wasn't in bad shape, but it was obvious that it was used and abused. I should have figured as much but didn't. I didn't know what I expected.

"Help me unhook so we can go," Stu said, nodding to the deck. I smiled in return and followed him. We pulled the ropes from their anchors on the dock and

Stu started her up. It'd been a really long time since I'd been on a boat, but this one sounded like she was cared for. She purred.

"At least she's been maintained," I said. Stu nodded his agreement and drove away.

Twenty-Two

We were already in the Atlantic but still had a way to go. Only a handful of miles total, but even at a speed equivalent to fifty miles per hour, it still took twenty minutes. Clearly, I'd held the impression that the Gulf Stream was much farther out than it was.

When we arrived, Stu cut the engine, and I went below to get some rope and gloves from my bag.

"Whoa! I had no idea all that was in there," Stu remarked.

"It's heavier than it looks. There's still more in there," I said with a smirk. "I don't think you want to know, do you?"

Stu shook his head. "No, I guess not. But the curiosity will get to me one day." He grinned.

I nodded at the fish's dinner, and Stu came down. I went back up. Stu followed, Andrew over his shoulder. Stu laid the body down, and I cut the bag that was around the top half of Andrew just enough for the blood to be visible through the plastic wrapper I'd made him.

I smiled proudly. "Maybe if you'd learned how to treat women, this wouldn't have happened." I looked at Stu, who stared at me, unsure what to think. I looked back down at Andrew as I cut the plastic. "Nah. You'd still be dead. Goodbye, sleaze bag."

I nodded to Stu and grabbed under Andrew's shoulders. Stu grabbed the end with his feet. We set him on the side of the boat so I could finish making the necessary cuts in the bags and plastic. The cuts made it easier for the fish and sharks to know what was there for them to snack on.

Stu stepped back, watching me. When I'd made the final cut and slid his cell phone in with the body, I pushed what used to be Andrew into the water. He bobbed for a minute or so, then began to sink. I hadn't weighted the bags because the research I'd done when I killed Shae stated it wasn't always necessary, that bodies only float after about a week. In that time, I'd expected there wouldn't be much, if anything, left of him.

Stu came over next to me and watched as Sleaze drifted deeper and deeper down. Then he was out of sight.

Stu looked at me. "Now what?"

"We wait for another thirty minutes. To be sure he doesn't come popping back up. Then we can go." I said staring into the water where Andrew had disappeared.

Stu pulled me to him. I looked into his eyes as he looked into mine. "Thank you for letting me help."

"You're welcome?" I wasn't sure how to respond, and it came out sounding like a question.

He kissed me—long, hard, and passionate. "I'm kind of turned on by you right now."

"Right now? Kind of?" I laughed. "I see how it is." I kissed him back. We held each other for a few minutes until I checked my watch. "We can go now. I don't see him."

"Okay," Stu said and released me. "Back to land and your house."

"Oh?" I arched an eyebrow, and my expression was barely visible in the yellowish light that emanated up from below deck combined with the bit of moon that shone.

Stu winked, started the engine, and turned us around, bound for home. Well, not quite home but back to land. Then home.

We docked and anchored, tethering the boat. Before covering it back up, I tossed my bag onto the dock.

Getting the last snaps of the cover in place was difficult—more so than I expected. It also took longer seeing how it didn't want to fully stretch. It fought me so hard, I'd almost lost a fingernail to it.

"Fucking *whore*!" I yelled, grabbing my fingertip. It throbbed and pulsed, and I thought for sure the nail was missing. Stu came over to me and gingerly unwrapped my hand from my finger.

He smiled and looked up at me. "You're gonna be fine. No blood. But it'll probably bruise really badly." He kissed it and helped me snap the cover into place.

"Fuck that cover," I said. "I'll bet it's brand new, too, and that's why it's uncooperative."

Stu chuckled. "Well, we're done now anyway. You ready to go home?"

I smiled and nodded as I picked my bag up and slung it over my shoulder. "You bet! This high won't wear off until later, I'm sure. You're coming with me, right?"

Stu just smiled and kissed me.

I jumped in my Jeep and tossed the bag onto the floor behind my seat. Stu got into his car and followed me all the way back. We took the interstate just because it was faster at this hour. And because Stu's car looked like an undercover police car, having him behind my Jeep benefited both of us.

I parked in my garage and Stu pulled into my driveway shortly after. As he closed the door, he looked to the old lady's house. All the inside lights were off, but the outside lights were on. That was her usual. It was mine too. But I didn't sit like a fucking creeper and watch through the window. I reached out for Stu's hand, and we walked to the front door.

"She really is a piece of work," Stu said. "Is she on your list?"

"You know nothing of serial killers, huh?" I said, unlocking and opening the door.

"I do too. Well…alright…No, not really. Mainly just the fictional ones you seem to idolize," he said with a chuckle.

"I don't *idolize* them. They're useful, is all. I don't have to use one of them as research so much because his character was a narcissist who ultimately gave himself up. *I have no intentions of doing that.* Though he did have an iconic kill scene. I could only hope to be that creative." I cackled.

Stu closed and locked the door. Then he kissed me. "Time to go to bed?" There was a mischievous twinkle in his eye.

I led the way upstairs. Stu undressed as we walked. When we reached the bedroom, I set the bag down in my closet near the safe. Stu was already on the bed, shirtless, when I turned around. I smiled wickedly and leaped onto him. He caught me.

We made out like horny teenagers. But the sex was more than that. We connected so completely—on a soul level—that I cried. Stu seemed to know why because he didn't ask. He just held me tighter.

When we were finished, I lay there staring at the ceiling for a few minutes. We didn't need to talk. We understood what each other was feeling. I rolled over and slid off the bed, intent to shower. That was the only thing that could make me feel any more euphoric than I already did. It seemed to be a normal post-kill thing for me. Plus, the sea air made my skin feel gross, and after the heated lovemaking, my skin was that much stickier.

Stu joined me in soaping the salty air from my pores, washing the ocean off of our bodies. Then, we toweled off and went to bed. I wasn't sure I'd ever been so happy to go to sleep. Or for a Saturday morning.

Twenty-Three

WE WOKE AROUND 2 p.m. feeling refreshed in every possible way. I rolled onto my side to face Stu. We stared at each other for what felt like hours.

Stu blinked first. "Hungry?"

"Actually, yeah. I'll make the coffee. You cook?"

"Sounds like a plan."

I slid out of bed and threw my pajamas on before going to the bathroom to brush my teeth. Stu put his underwear back on and followed.

"Whea rr ur cwoves?" I tried to ask while brushing.

Stu laughed and nodded. They were magically laid out on the bed; I hadn't seen them on my walk past that side of the bed.

"I grabbed them before coming in here," he said after rinsing.

I rinsed. "Oh," I replied. "I knew I wasn't hallucinating."

Just then, I heard what sounded like a small elephant running up the stairs. It was followed by a shrill meow. Stu and I looked at each other, shocked such a loud noise could come from such a small cat. Stu scooped Minion up and petted her.

"I'll feed her," he said setting her on the bed so he could pull his pants on. I watched like a voyeur. He stood, turning to face me.

"Tsk, tsk, Ms. Cage," he said, using his fingers to make the *shame, shame* motion I hadn't seen since childhood.

I laughed. Stu kissed me then went downstairs, Minion following like a puppy. At least I didn't have to worry if my child liked my boyfriend. I shrugged and slid my feet into slippers before going downstairs.

Stu was already at the stove, making what looked like eggs and I didn't know what else. I didn't ask either. Instead, I focused on making coffee as my brain threatened to start a revolution if it didn't receive caffeine soon.

I didn't even wait for the pot to fill, and pulled the carafe from the burner when there was enough of the soul juice for a cup. I slid the carafe back on and sipped.

"Ah!" I screamed, nearly dropping the mug.

"You okay?" Stu asked, turning around to check on me.

"Yeah. In my need for caffeine, I forgot to add ice cubes so this didn't happen." I grunted as I walked to the freezer and pulled out three ice cubes. Then I plunked them into the mug, not caring that I'd spilled coffee all around the mug on the countertop. I wiped it up with a paper towel while the cubes melted.

Then I sipped again. "Much better," I said.

Stu made a noise that sounded like a snort and laugh combined. "Want some?"

"Please," he replied. "But no ice."

"Hah," I said as I poured him a mug. I set it on the counter next to him rather than interrupt him cooking.

He picked it up between bouts of stirring and drank. "Thanks," he said.

"Of course. Anything I can do to help?"

"Yeah, get out of the kitchen," he said with a smile. "I don't need you burning yourself again, klutz."

"It's about damned time *somebody* appreciated that fact about me," I said then erupted into giggle fits. "It may not be that funny to you, but I think it's that funny. Probably because I know the depths of my klutziness. You're still learning."

I giggled some more on my way out to the couch. As I sat down, I turned the TV on and flipped through the streaming apps. A couple of them offered live shows, and I chose the one I watched the most. I had a thing for home remodeling shows; they gave me ideas of what I wanted in my next house, should there be one. With Stu and I together, I might allow myself to eventually start thinking about a future and us getting our own place. Which would likely be a bigger house.

I'd finished my first mug and gotten up to get more. Stu smiled at me while he pulled something out of the oven. I avoided looking because I'd probably trip over nothing this time and didn't want to commit more coffee abuse.

"I was thinking," Stu started as I poured, "bacon seems to be your favorite, judging by your freezer. But how do you feel about bacon *and* sausage?"

I refilled his empty mug. "Why not? I have nothing against more meat. But I also don't know what you're making, so I can't…Ah, fuck it. You have free rein," I said.

Stu turned to me, pan in both mitt-covered hands. "I'm glad you said that"—he lowered his face and sniffed the frittata—"because I already put both in here."

I joined him in sniffing, and my mouth started to water. "Damn, that smells amazing!"

"Doesn't it?" Stu wore a proud expression as he set the skillet on a pot holder so he wouldn't burn the countertop. I took some paper plates down from a cabinet and a knife from the block. Stu grinned like a child.

We cut it up and ate half of our first pieces before leaving the kitchen. When we realized that, we smirked and plated more. Then we went into the living room and watched more home improvement shows.

My phone rang shortly after I'd swallowed my last mouthful. It was Joe Osten.

"Hey, Joe! What's up?"

"I'm calling to tell you that Marsha has decided to have dinner with us. She has one request: that it be the four of us. She enjoys making larger meals and knows I don't do leftovers much," he said.

"Mhm," I muttered. "I'll bet she just doesn't want to feel like a third wheel."

"That too," Joe replied. "So? Will you and Stu join us?"

"Of course! When?"

"How does tonight sound?"

I looked at Stu. "Hang on, I'll ask him now," I told Joe.

"Ask me what?" Stu asked.

"Dinner. Joe's. Tonight."

"I don't see why not," he said, shrugging.

"We'll be there," I said to Joe.

"Great! See you at seven. Oh! Don't even think about trying to be slick again," he said with a chuckle.

"Yes, sir," I grumbled while wearing a grin.

Joe hung up, and I looked over at Stu. He smiled at me and kissed my cheek.

Things seemed to be moving in the right direction.

Twenty-Four

WE ARRIVED AT JOE'S house a little before seven. Stu rang the bell, and Joe answered so fast it was almost as if he'd been waiting there.

"Britney!" Joe was happier than usual and hugged me as I walked in. "Stu," he said, reaching out to shake hands.

Stu shook back, matching Joe's happiness.

It was a strange thing that both men were so happy. I wanted to say they were high, but that wasn't true. At least not of Stu. Though Stu's reason for this extreme happiness was something more familiar to me: we'd loved each other for so long and now we were together.

"Joe, you're happier than usual," I commented. "What's the occasion?"

"Nothing, really. I'm just happy for you." He winked at Stu, but spoke to me.

I nodded. "I see," I said, smirking. "You men are like children." I joked.

"That we are. At least right now," Stu replied.

Marsha was setting the table when we reached the dining room. She smiled at us. "Dinner will be ready shortly," she said.

"How about I help you finish setting up?" I said more than asked. Marsha smiled at me but didn't reply. I took that as a yes and followed her into the kitchen.

"It's great to see you," she said to me.

I hugged her. "You too. I'm glad you decided to join us. Now we can get to know each other better. After all, you take really good care of Joe, and I know how difficult he can be."

Marsha giggled. "He can be a handful. And I was the oldest of six, so that's saying something!"

I cringed and giggled at the same time. The merging of those two actions hurt my body as much as my brain. "That's…wow. I don't know whether to apologize or congratulate you."

Martha smiled. "Thanks. Joe is still easier than helping raise five other kids when you're just a kid yourself."

I picked up a stack of plates that sat on the island and headed for the dining room. "I can only imagine."

"Enough about my childhood," Marsha said uncomfortably as she followed me carrying napkins and utensils.

We set each place setting on the table and kept talking.

"I decided to be a housekeeper—or caretaker?—for people like Joe because I genuinely enjoy the job," she said, her green eyes sparkling. "I learned from taking care of my dad when he got older. Sadly, he got too sick too fast. My mother was devastated. So was I. It was a bad time for my family, but we got through it. Anyway, Joe has quickly become my favorite." She smiled.

Stu, Joe, and I chuckled. "Why's that?" I asked.

"Because he's a genuinely nice guy. And he's funny." She blushed being put on the spot like that.

"That's enough, Britney," Joe said with a smile. "I won't have you torturing my helper."

No, Joe, I wouldn't do that. I'm not that stupid.

"Who me? Never!" I feigned hurt then laughed. "Come on, Marsha. Let's get these fools something to drink and talk about them." I winked and put my arm around her shoulders. She giggled as we walked through the door to the kitchen.

"I see why he loves you so much," Marsha commented as I plucked a bottle of Riesling from the wine fridge.

"Why *who* loves me?" I asked, perplexed.

"Joe," she responded thoughtfully. "And Stu. I guess both of them."

I giggled uncomfortably. "But why do you say that?"

She turned the stove off and took the pot off the burner. "You're sweet, kind, caring, and funny."

If you only knew. It was my turn to blush. "Thanks. You're pretty cool yourself."

We took the wine and food out to the dining room. I poured everyone a glass and lifted mine in toast. "To having everyone together," I said.

"Cheers," everyone else responded.

I sipped then helped Marsha retrieve the rest of the food she'd prepared and set it out on the table.

We sat across from each other, each of us at either of Joe's elbows. We enjoyed good food, good conversation, and good people. Marsha was funny and sweet and nice. I imagined having her join me and my friends for a girls' night. But we could be crude, and I wasn't sure Marsha would approve. I resolved to get to know her better first. Then I'd decide if she'd be a good fit. I hoped she would be. Something told me she'd get along famously with Danielle.

When we finished one bottle of wine, I stood to get another. Marsha stood too. "I'm closer to the door. I'll get it," she said.

I chose not to argue and sat back down. Joe looked at me funny.

"What?" I asked.

"Normally, you'd insist that you help. You must be learning to pick your battles," he remarked.

"I don't know about this being a *battle*…"

"You get what I'm saying," Joe said before sipping the remaining wine in his glass.

Marsha returned and poured more in everyone's glasses. We thanked her as she sat back down.

I was a little annoyed by Joe's comment, but I was trying my hardest to let it slide. I'd talk to Stu about it on the way back to my house. He'd make me see that my annoyance was unnecessary.

Once we were all stuffed, Marsha and I cleared the table while Stu and Joe talked again, presumably about me. It was narcissistic of me to think that's all they had to talk about. It turned out they actually had more in common. When we came back in with dessert and plates, they were discussing football teams.

Stu laughed maniacally about the two big shots that Joe's favorite team had acquired during the off-season.

"One of them destroyed his phone so he wouldn't be caught cheating," Stu chided.

"Oh boy," I muttered under my breath to Marsha. She shot me an *uh-oh* glance, and we giggled.

"Ha! When was the last time your team even made the playoffs?" Joe shot back, laughing.

"Children," I said. "Fight nicely."

Joe looked at me. "You hush. You like the same team he does." Then he chuckled.

I sighed. "At least my team admitted they used drugs." We all laughed at that.

"Makes me wish they did again. Maybe then we'd get another Super Bowl," Stu joked.

I giggled and said, "My sentiments exactly."

We took jabs at each other's teams for the remainder of dessert and the cups of coffee that followed. Stu looked at his watch and blanched.

"I start day shift tomorrow, and it's getting late. We should be going," he said looking over at me.

I nodded and stood. "Let me help clean up," I said to Marsha.

"Nonsense. Give me a hug and get out of here." She apparently understood a reason why Stu had wanted to leave now that I didn't, aside from needing his beauty sleep.

I did as she asked, and Joe walked us to the door.

"Thanks again for having us," Stu said, reaching to shake Joe's hand.

Joe wrapped him in a hug. "I'll have none of that. You're family now. Be good to her," he said, then hugged me. "And you be good to him."

Stu and I nodded in unison. "We will," I replied. Stu opened the door, and we walked to my Jeep.

"I think I'll go home tonight. You know, give you a break from me," Stu said as I drove off.

"Yeah, we wouldn't want that. Especially since we know what happens to those who get on my nerves."

Twenty-Five

Stu got in his car and left after a long kiss good-night. I was really considering giving him a key but still wasn't sold on the idea.

I went inside, fed Minion, and changed for bed. When I lay down, I found myself missing having a warm body next to me. I missed cuddling.

So, I turned the TV on and waited for my eyelids to get heavy. This new way of falling asleep was unacceptable, and I vowed to figure out another way, even if that meant CBD or something. As long as it wasn't prescribed…

• • • • • • • • • • •

I stopped to grab lattes on my way into the office again. Maybe it was becoming a regular thing. I didn't mind it but didn't want it to continue. It signaled that I wasn't getting enough sleep and that was unaccept-able.

When I walked in, I lowered my arm so Barb could grab hers from the carrier.

"Thanks," she said. "Long night?"

I snickered. "Not in the way you're thinking." I giggled in spite of myself. "I really think I need to start smoking or something." Then I saw the look on her face. "Oh! Not cigarettes! Sorry. I meant green stuff to smoke."

Barb was sipping from her cup, so she nodded. Then said, "Oh! Thanks for the clarification! For a second there, I was thinking about throwing my coffee at you."

"That's drastic," I commented as I walked into my office. Barb followed.

"Well of course it is. You come in here talking about starting a smoking habit. How else am I supposed to react?"

I booted up. "Fair enough. Sorry again. I didn't mean to worry you." *Jesus! And sometimes I think I'm crazy!*

Barb looked at me, a thoughtful expression on her face. "I care about you, that's all. I don't want to see you hurt yourself." Then she walked out.

I chewed my lower lip as I typed. I was sorry I'd freaked her out. I also didn't think there was a way to make it up to her. I'd apologized, and that would have to be enough. I was sure it had been. She'd get over it, wouldn't she?

I'd lost track of time having gotten lost in a deluge of emails. The only reason I'd even looked at all was because my phone rang. It was just before noon.

"Passing Thr—"

"Britney, it's Jim."

"Hey, Jim, you okay?"

"Yeah, sure. Look, Andrew quit. I'm sorry to be calling you so late about it; it's been a busy morning. See, on Friday, he gave me two weeks' notice. But then he didn't show up today, so I got stuck doing his work too. Anyway, I guess I'll need someone else as soon as you can swing it."

A malevolent smile spread across my face while Jim spoke.

"He did call me and leave a message saying he needed to talk. But he didn't answer when I called him back. Not that this is anything strange. He's pulled crap like this before. Not ever with me. But at a job he had where he and his sole coworker didn't get along… Anyway, I'll look into who we've got available and send them your way. Any preference what day they start?"

"No. Just as soon as possible, please. I knew Andrew was a weirdo, but damn," he said. "Oh! And you remember Barb and I are moving next weekend, right? We're having a party the week after too. But I only say something because she's been so overwhelmed…Did she remember to request off for next Friday?"

I couldn't tell if Jim was controlling or overbearing or just concerned. So I lied. "Yeah, she did. I've got it here on the calendar already."

Jim sighed. "Good. The poor girl's been a fruit loop lately. Okay, I gotta get back to it. Thanks, Britney!"

"No problem. Chat soon."

When Jim hung up, I wasn't sure what to think about what he said. Was I over-analyzing? Projecting? It couldn't have been jealousy; Stu was the same way with me. Well, maybe not quite so strong when talking about me, but essentially the same otherwise.

"Barb?"

"Yes?" She walked to the doorway.

"You're moving next weekend, right?" I wasn't prodding, but it sounded that way.

"Ah! Yes. Ohmigod! I forgot to—"

"You didn't. You reminded me last week. I've got it on my calendar. Party the following weekend." I smiled. "You have that Friday off for your move."

Barb relaxed and sighed, her shoulders slumping a bit. "I'm so glad one of us remembered. It's been a long month and change. I've been so busy lately, I really did forget. And how could I possibly forget? Not that I forgot I'm moving, that I forgot to check if I asked you for that Friday off…" She sat in the chair across from me, looking worn out.

"Barb," I said calmly. "You're fine. Stop rambling, though, I'm having trouble keeping up. Anyway, look, if you need more time off, just let me know. I'll still pay you for it. You've earned that much. Can I ask you something about Jim?"

She straightened, confused. "Sure. Is everything alright?"

I smiled. "Sure is. I just got a little concerned when he made sure you had asked for the day off. He's not…controlling or anything, is he?"

Barb chuckled. "No! Oh wow! No, he just comes off that way. Kinda like you do."

I arched an eyebrow. "I do?"

Barb blanched. She hated confrontation. "I mean…well…"

"I wish someone had told me before now. I'll work on it. Can you just tell me when I'm acting like that?" I asked. I was lying. I had no plans to try anything. I knew I was domineering at times; it was part of who I was. But she'd opened that door, and there was no going back now.

"Um, sure. I can do that," Barb answered, but I knew she wouldn't tell me. I had to make it seem like I was aware it was a problem.

"Sorry to put you on the spot like that," I said.

"No worries," she said, standing. "I'm going to lunch. Be back in an hour."

That conversation had been a little more awkward and weirder than I'd expected, but Barb and I were both awkward in our own ways. I accepted that.

I also accepted that time moved faster on Mondays. The next thing I knew, the day was over, and I was in my pajamas on my couch. It was as though I'd done a shit ton of drugs and my high ended here. Where had the day gone?

I went to the kitchen to pour a glass of wine, only to discover there was none left. I was really slacking. First, the lack of sleep, then no wine in the house. I'd become my own problem. *You're losing it, Brit. Get it together, or you'll lose everything.*

My phone rang, stopping the ominous thoughts. The screen told me it was Stu.

"How much do you love me?" I asked as I answered.

"Well, hello to you too," Stu said with a chuckle. "To eternity. What do you need me to bring with me?"

He knew me too well. "Wine. Like two or three bottles. I'll pay for dinner in exchange."

"This isn't a business thing, Brit," Stu said sounding offended.

"You know what I meant," I said defensively.

He chuckled. "I did. I was kidding about being offended. I love you, Britney Cage," he said and hung up.

I almost swooned as I set the phone back down on the coffee table. Could I really be so lucky? I didn't think I was. And being skeptical was my nature. I killed people who deserved it for one reason or another. Most were annoyances in my life, but Andrew hadn't been just for me. I'd killed him for women everywhere; one less slime-ball to worry about.

I tried hard to stop being cynical about how good Stu was to me. He was a genuine soul who genuinely loved me. That would have to be enough. And it was. For my heart. My brain was a matter all by itself.

Stu knocked on my front door forty minutes later. I opened the door, and he kissed me hello. I tried to take the bag of wine from him, but he wasn't having it. So I followed him into the kitchen and snagged a bottle of moscato as he slid it into the fridge.

"Not a fan of cold wine?" Stu smirked.

"Actually, no. Moscato doesn't need to be cold or chilled for me. Room temperature works just fine," I said, pulling two glasses down from the cabinet.

"I have beer," Stu said, holding out a bottle of Bud Light.

I nodded and put a glass back, then twisted the top from his bottle.

"Thanks," he said. "I'd have gotten that."

I smiled and poured my glass of wine.

We sat at the kitchen table across from each other. "What are we eating?" I asked.

Stu swigged his beer. "The age-old question." He joked. "Burgers? Pizza? Mexican?"

"Ooh! Mexican!" I ran to grab my phone from the living room so I could check which restaurant had the shortest wait time for delivery. When I got back, Stu had already had his out and was scrolling through.

"Lolis is open!" I squealed.

Stu nodded and chuckled, then gave me his order. I read our choices back then pressed the order button. The app told me our dinner should arrive within the hour.

Stu grabbed himself another beer and poured me more wine. We clinked and went to sit on the couch and cuddle while watching my favorite meteorologist.

Less than forty-five minutes later, the bell rang. Stu stood to get our food. It was the same delivery person who'd shown up last time I ordered food. I waved to her and thanked her. Then I checked the app to make sure I'd left a good tip.

Stu took the bag to the kitchen and I followed. He took our food out, and I grabbed us some plates, napkins, and silverware. Stu plated his food and offered to plate mine. I shook my head, choosing to do it myself. He waited for me to finish and we sat at the kitchen table to eat.

The night passed like I'd imagined one would if we were an old, married couple. It was kind of nice. I'd wondered if it were something I could get used to.

We hung out on the couch and watched a movie until we were tired enough to go to sleep. On our way upstairs, Stu blindsided me with a question.

Twenty-Six

"WHEN DO YOU WANT to exchange keys?"

"Huh?" I asked, unable to form words. I'd almost expected him to be asking something much different.

"Well, I want you to have a key to my place and was thinking, since I'm here so much…"

"Oh! Yeah…I mean…yeah. I'll have one made for you, but do you think now is the right time? Shouldn't we get used to just being together first?"

Stu sat on the bed, wearing a blank expression. It appeared he hadn't anticipated resistance.

"I didn't think of it that way," he admitted. "I guess I kinda just assumed you'd be okay with it."

I shrugged as I pulled the comforter back. "I want to be. I really do. But given my history with dating…"

My eyes met his. They pleaded with mine to see his bare soul, that he was genuine and real and nothing to be afraid of.

"I know I have no reason to be concerned, but let me ask you. When was the last time you were in a serious relationship?" I asked him.

Stu thought about that for a few minutes as we both lay down and got comfortable. He still hadn't spoken by the time I'd turned a movie on to fall asleep to. And I didn't want to pressure him, so I kept my mouth shut.

Then Stu sat up on his elbow and looked at me. "It's been a long time," he said then kissed me. "This is the first time you've told me no that I find myself agreeing with." He lay back down and pulled me close.

"Thank you," I said. "I just need some time to get used to having a boyfriend. I haven't been in a committed relationship since…Well, it's been a long time. I love you, Stewart Jones." I kissed his chest where his heart would be and gently stroked his face. Then I laid my head back on my pillow and fell asleep.

As I drifted off, I heard Stu say, "I love you too, Britney Cage."

I awoke on my side with Stu's arm draped over me. The sun was hidden behind a cloudy sky, casting a dim light into my bedroom. I smiled. I was happy that things worked out the way they had. Stu and I were happy, and we had an unspoken agreement that we'd remain that way, no matter the cost. I wanted it to stay that way forever. Could it?

I got up and went about my usual routine, with Stu joining me for my jog. More than once, my heart told me that I could get used to this. My brain agreed half the time. The other half, it argued with itself. The arguments ranged from paranoid to logical, with the major fear being the repeat of history with an addition. The addition of me being caught and sentenced to death. I saw the argument taking some time to calm down and reconcile. Stu seemed to understand my hesitation in that regard, as well.

When we got back, Stu made coffee while I showered and got ready. It was a nice thing—to have someone helping make sure your day started off right. I knew it wouldn't always be sunshine and roses, but it was still a good feeling.

We'd parted ways with a kiss and the words *I love you, be safe*. I knew firsthand that taking one's personal safety for granted was a bad idea. Stu knew it too. That was why we both said it.

Barb was a literal ray of sunshine when I walked in.

"Morning, Brit!" She practically exploded with happiness.

I side-eyed her. "Hi, Barb. You okay?"

She practically pounced on me and hugged me. "We're all packed! Tomorrow starts the big move!"

If she's gonna be this happy all day, I'm gonna fucking slit her throat.

I smiled. "I almost forgot!"

Barb's face dropped.

"I'm kidding," I said. "I didn't forget. I just didn't think you'd be this excited. Last I knew, you were incredibly nervous."

Barb blushed. "I know. I called Julie last week because, well, I was hoping I'd just stop being so nervous. Anyway, she helped me calm down and be happy for myself. You were so right. Thanks for telling me to call her."

I nodded. "Of course. Now, could you please maybe not shriek so loud?" I plugged an ear with a pinkie finger and shook it around. "I'm afraid I'll go deaf." I was half joking, but Barb didn't seem to notice.

"Ohmigod! I'm so sorry!" Her face turned tomato red with embarrassment.

"Relax, it's not *that* serious," I said to her as I hung my purse on the rack inside my office door. "If you want, leave at lunch. I'm sure you could use the few extra hours…"

"You mean it? I mean, we've gotten everything together. Though I do think—"

"It's settled. Leave at lunch to finish what you have to," I finished and smiled.

Barb started to run at my desk—in an attempt to attack-hug me again, I assumed—but I stopped her by holding my hand up. She nodded and thanked me before going back to her desk.

I sat down and got to work myself. Mainly, I prepped myself to work from home for the afternoon and all of tomorrow. I expected it to be a decent change of pace. Not to mention the forecast looked ideal for working outside on my patio.

Noontime rolled around, and Barb came in to say goodbye. She had tears in her eyes.

"What's wrong?" I asked her.

"Nothing." She sniffed. "I'm just so grateful for you and so happy to be so happy…" She broke into sobs then sniffled and wiped her nose with a tissue. "Sorry. I can be overly emotional sometimes." She laughed at herself.

"I can see that," I said smiling. "Go. Have a great move. Let me know if you need anything."

"Thanks, Britney. We really appreciate it. You've already done so much for the two of us already. We couldn't ask for anything more."

"Pssh." I made a noise trying to cover up that I felt my face flush a little. "Let me know if you need anything," I repeated.

"I will." Bard hugged me and left.

I sighed, relieved that I was alone. Barb's happiness had emanated from the reception area and annoyed the hell out of me to the point that I thought I might have made her leave earlier. But I didn't exactly know how to tactfully send her home for being too happy.

I finished writing the emails I needed to reply to and packed up for the day. Then I set the call forwarding to my cell phone and locked up. I jumped into my Jeep and started her up.

My cell phone rang from inside my purse.

Twenty-Seven

I GROANED AND LET it go to voicemail. I drove out of the lot, and it rang again. I looked at the screen in the dash to see an unknown number. If I'd still been at the office, I would have had to answer it. So I did.

"Passing Through Temp Agency, Britney speaking." I answered.

"Brit! It's me, Jim. Is Barb still there?"

"No, she went home to finalize some details for the move tomorrow. Is everything okay?"

"Yeah. I just wanted to see if she wanted to grab lunch with me. No worries. Thanks," he said.

"Jim! Before you go…I have a new temp set up to start next week. I told her Monday, but I can push it back if you need me to."

"No, no. Monday's perfect! Thanks again, Brit. Have a great weekend!"

"Thanks, Jim. You too. If you need anything, call me."

"Will do," he said.

I hung up as I pulled into the Wawa parking lot. A hoagie sounded like perfection right about then.

When I got home, I was starving and looking forward to eating. First, though, I changed into comfy pants and a T-shirt. Working from home didn't mean I had to stay in an uncomfortable pencil skirt.

Then I set myself up to eat my lunch before finishing work outside on the patio. I ate and watched as the ducks quacked and sat around lazily. I still had plenty of bird feed, so I took some out to them before ending my workday.

The sun had never really come out from behind the curtain of clouds it hid behind, but the day grew significantly darker by the time I'd closed the laptop for the day. I smiled in spite of it; it was finally cool and dry enough out here to enjoy it. I sat until the streetlights came on and my doorbell rang.

"Be right there!" I called. There was no reply.

When I got to the door, I looked through the peephole. There was a patrol car in the driveway and the officer was standing back too far for me to tell if it was Stu or someone else.

I opened the door with a painted-on smile. The officer stepped closer to the door. It was Stu.

"Technically I'm here on official business," he started. "I need to tell you that Andrew York is missing. I also need to tell you that there have been multiple sexual harassment claims filed against him over the years. You'll likely be questioned, but there are plenty other women who may have wanted him gone." He smirked and kissed me.

"That was an official kiss," I said with a grin.

"That was the last official thing I needed you for," he replied, kissing me again.

"Want to come in?" I asked.

He shook his head. "When I get done. I just wanted to tell you in person, ma'am." He waved, got in the car, and left.

I closed the door and laughed. Had it really been so easy to get away with murder? Had it ever been diffi-cult…at all? Would it get easier? I still had so many questions and the only answer was that time would tell.

About two hours later, there was another knock on the door. It was Stu again. This time he wouldn't be leaving until the next morning. He greeted me with a kiss.

"Let's go out to dinner," he said.

I stared at him deadpan. "Really? You want to be around other people?"

"That's not what I was getting at," he retorted.

"Where did you have in mind?" I wasn't totally sold on going somewhere when we could easily order for pick-up.

"Outback," he replied. "It's been a while since I've had steak, let alone gone out to dinner."

I sighed. "Agreed. Okay, let me put some jeans on, and we'll go."

Stu grinned and kissed me. "Awesome. No dishes!"

I giggled and changed. When I came back down, Stu practically ran out the door.

"Whoa! Who's driving?" I asked, grabbing my purse and keys.

Stu raised his hand and walked out. I shook my head and smirked. *Boys will be boys.*

The drive north was horrible. It was rush hour, and everyone was headed home in a hurry. There had also been more than one fender bender. The cars didn't even bother to move from the drive lanes. *Assholes.*

When we arrived, we were told there was a wait of forty-five minutes.

"We should have called on the way here. Might have been able to get a table sooner," I said.

Stu nodded. "Didn't even cross my mind."

"Mine either. No worries," I said and kissed his cheek.

We sat on a bench outside and enjoyed just sitting next to one another in the cool breeze. I rested my head on his shoulder until I heard my name. I looked at Stu.

"Did we give them my name?"

"I don't think so," he replied.

I looked around, not seeing the hostess. I didn't think they had pagers either, since the waiting area was so small. Then I heard my name again.

This time, a woman walked up to me. I didn't recognize her at first. She had a fit build, blonde hair, and blue eyes. She had two little girls with her, which threw me off even more. I couldn't recall knowing anyone who looked like her, let alone who had two small children.

"Britney, it's me, Becca Martin. I worked for you when you first opened. You sent me to Dr. Osten's office. I quit because his patients hated me. Remember?"

My face betrayed my thoughts. She stepped back, a little scared.

"It's starting to come back to me," I lied, and straightened my face to match my words.

A man walked up to Becca and kissed her cheek. "I'm sorry! Where are my manners? This is my husband, Bobby. And these are our nieces."

I waved. "Nice to meet you," I said. "This is my boyfriend, Stu."

Stu greeted them politely.

"Well, it was good to see you," Becca said. "We should meet up for coffee or something to catch up one of these days."

"Sounds great," I replied. "You know how to reach me."

They walked away and Stu looked at me. He knew I had no clue who that woman was. I shook my head and giggled.

The hostess called Stu's name, and we stood to walk in.

"Man, I thought I was going to have to eat a person," I commented on our walk inside. Stu agreed.

The hostess took us to our table, and we sat down. Within minutes, our server arrived to take our drink order and walked away.

The night carried on with no further interruptions. Stu and I enjoyed our meals and each other's company. We even enjoyed being out.

I lifted my glass in toast. "Here's to not having to do dishes," I said.

"Cheers to that!" Stu replied. We clinked glasses and finished them off.

"Let's get out of here," I said with a smirk and a wink.

Stu gave the server cash and told her to keep the change. Knowing him, the tip had likely been more than most people would leave. We stood and walked out. I heard my name being called again.

Becca waved at us from her table. We waved back and kept walking.

Stu had just turned onto South Dale Mabry when it hit me. "I know exactly who that bitch was!"

"Who are you talking about? That Becca lady?" he asked.

"She's a fucking lying asshole. The betrayal…ugh!"

"That bad?"

"You have no idea," I grumbled. "I swore that if I ever saw her again, I'd rip her lying throat out."

"Well, I'm now glad you didn't remember her until now." Stu chuckled. "We wouldn't have been able to cover it up if you'd lost it."

Stu parked in my driveway, and we walked into the house before I said another word. I didn't need the nosy one hearing anything and thinking something totally wrong.

"I wouldn't have lost it on her. Not in public, anyway."

"I know," Stu said. "I was kidding."

"Heh." I went upstairs to change and came back down. We sat on the couch to watch an episode of some show Stu wanted me to see. When the episode was over, we went upstairs to bed.

"Bet you thought we were gonna have sex?" I said, turning the light off.

"Our relationship isn't all about that," Stu said sounding a little hurt. "But yeah, I kind of did. I mean, you did make that face when we were leaving the restaurant."

I kissed him. "Then I let my anger get the best of me. Forgive me?"

"How could I not?" He smiled.

We lay there in silence for a little while. Then Stu put another episode on. "I'm not that tired right now, "he admitted.

"Me either," I said. My mind was playing a different show. The one where Becca had betrayed every ounce of trust I'd given her so long ago.

That bitch and her perfect husband would be next.

Acknowledgments

This book, let alone series, wouldn't be possible without the following people and references:

Practical Homicide Investigation (5th Edition) by way of a Thomas Harris acknowledgement. The FBI's *Serial Murder Multi-Disciplinary Perspectives for Investigators* Report (available free online), and *psychologytoday.com* for helping me add the necessary depth to Britney.

Ret. Sgt. Chuck Burns for his consultation where the textbook didn't answer specific questions.

Justin D., for helping me on ridiculously short notice with some nicknames.

Nathan, for his advice and invitations. I'm so very grateful I finally decided to take you up.

Mark...sweet Mark. Without you, I wouldn't be here. I love you more than I can express and always will.

Jason, for the awesome editing and blurbs and feedback and advice and just being you. You have made me the writer I am today. Let's not get arrested, please. At least not before we make that money.

Also by Amanda Byrd

13 Reasons for Murder:
Politeness Kills (#1)
Meathead (#2)
Philistines (#3)
Hungry (#4)
Bad Blood (#5)
Betrayal (#6)
Disillusioned (#7)

The Morgan Davis Serials
The Girl at the Bottom of the Ocean (#1)
Before You Die (#2)

Anthologies
Thrill of the Hunt: Cabin Fever (Thrill of the Hunt Anthology Book 6)

The Dr. van Wolfe Saga
Trapped (book 1)
Moratorium (book 2)

Medicate (book 3)